REASON
FOR
EXISTENCE

Copyright 2016 by Richard Botelho
ISBN: 978-0-9643926-6-3 (softcover)
ISBN: 978-0-9643926-7-0 (ebook)
Library of Congress Control Number: 2015941176

Published by Windstream Publishing Company
303 Windstream Place, Danville, CA 94526
Manufactured in the United States of America
First Edition 2016

Publisher's Cataloging-in-Publication
(Provided by Quality Books, Inc.)

Botelho, Richard.

Reason for Existence : a novel / by Richard Botelho.

ISBN 978-0-9643926-6-3
ISBN 978-0-9643926-7-0

1. Spirituality--Fiction. 2. Science fiction.
PS3602.O86R43 2015   813'.6
QBI15-600098

For October of 2011

ACKNOWLEDGMENTS

I wish to thank the following people for their contribution to *Reason for Existence*, from those who made suggestions affecting style and structure, to those who contributed with their ideas and inspiration. To Lisa, Lindsey, and O'Brien Editorial for their honest critiques and comprehensive edits. To my many beta readers and early advisors who gave me such valuable insight and constructive criticism. Of course to my Mom and Dad. Also, to my many friends who have inspired me over the years with the living of their lives. And, as always, to Dr. Richard Hughes, Dr. George Tokmakoff, Dr. Charles Houghton and Dr. Clyde Enroth, all of California State University, Sacramento, for providing the best example of commitment to cause I have ever known. Lastly, to TheCreativePenn.com, TheBookDesigner.com, WorldLiteraryCafe.com, and BookMarket.com for being so incredibly informative and educational.

"Let all that you do be done in love."

1 Corinthians 16:14

REASON
FOR
EXISTENCE

A NOVEL

RICHARD BOTELHO

PROLOGUE

Associated Press—Beijing, China
September 2, 2017
The government of China today announced the beginning of military exer-
cises along its southern frontier, in a region stretching over 1,000 miles from
the Nepalese border to Vietnam, in what Western analysts are saying are
the largest such exercises in its history. Analysts note the exercises appear to
be a direct response to the Greater Asian Trade and Defense Pact (GATDP)
signed between the United States, India, Japan, the Philippines, Australia,
South Korea, and a host of other nations concerned with growing Chinese
assertiveness in the region.

Truth is found in the hills. Mine are in California, in the coastland ridges of Oakland, towering high above San Francisco Bay, yielding golden secrets in the sunlight like a peek into my eyes. Neither of us is what we seem. Like these hills I am a mystery. Still, there are lessons to be learned among the shadow breaks and drooping mists, for I feel it in my soul. Locals tell stories of finding passion and even love in these majestic wooded rises, but that seems as elusive to me as the occasional coyote seen yipping in my yard. Even the forest trails here are a riddle; many of the footpaths meander aimlessly and I have yet to find a satisfactory explanation for their bewildering arrangement and excursive convolution and seldom is there any reason for what happens here or why the grandest answers always come with pain.

I have sought meaning all my life. No, not for me, rather to understand the people of this Earth, the mothers and fathers and sons and daughters who have proceeded from generation to generation in search of their destiny, who have surmounted so much and who surmount so much to this very day. It is impossible to live among the people and not feel some affinity for their struggles. But it is equally impossible to ignore contempt for their darkest hours. I have seen their hearts break while burying their precious ones in the ground, yet I have seen them make war on each other and drop fire from the sky. I have seen babies burned and women raped and families slaughtered to no avail, yet I have seen the tender times of lovers and the charity of the poor. I have seen the sallow, disbelieving faces of an ethnic cleansing stumble forth from camps of living hell and I have seen courts of justice hold the wicked to account. I have seen men and women of supposed reason deny their hands across the aisle while the innocents they serve pray their gods to grant wisdom to the wise. I have seen folly. I have seen lies. I have most certainly seen evil. But I have also seen humanitarians sacrifice their lives for a principle truest to their soul or politicians dedicate themselves in service for an ideal they admire. I have seen hope lost and hope gained and I have witnessed the tearful pleas for higher natures and the will to start again anew. The people of this land are a strange people, yet they possess a perseverance all their own, a perseverance like the hills themselves, unflagging and contrary to the evidence clearly in plain view. Humans disappoint as much as they inspire and they fail as much as they succeed. Still, something propels them forward, something I've never quite understood about the people living here. So in lockstep with the hills that are my home, my curiosity grows through the years as I observe the world below in nightly glow and daily ponder the human way.

ONE

Associated Press—San Francisco, United States
September 2, 2017

The government of Japan today lodged a formal complaint against the Chinese government for two separate violations of its territorial waters involving Chinese destroyers. The incidents were said to occur about ten miles northwest of Matsue on the island of Honshu and eight miles northeast of Saga on the island of Kyushu. The Japanese also claim that a third ship, rumored to be a spying vessel, was seen in the latter of the two incidents before speeding away into open ocean waters. The Chinese government has refused to comment on the alleged incidents.

I ambled in the woods near my mountain home one bright and surprisingly fogless September morning, when my cell phone rang with an anxious Nicholas Straka on the line.

"David?"

"Yes, Nicholas, how good to hear from you." His Greek accent and barrel baritone were unmistakable. So was the wisecrack he was about to make.

"You still watch the evening news, don't you?" Nicholas cracked sarcastically. "You'd think with the world on the verge of nuclear Armageddon you might offer your assistance for a change."

"Oh brother, here comes an ear full."

"Stop your whining. I'm the Secretary General of the United Nations and long your best friend in life. Or have you forgotten from whence you came?"

"You're not about to lecture me on the virtues of redistributive economics, are you?" I asked him, only half jokingly. "Tell me I'm spared your contribution to Marxism-Leninism on this otherwise so splendid a day."

"You could use some proletarian consciousness. You've made millions on the backs of the unfortunate poor."

"Okay, fine, I'll donate." I was still rather lighthearted and absorbed in the wonder of my view. "How much of my money do you need?"

"No, I don't want your money this time, I need your help. The way I see it, you owe me."

I couldn't believe his last comment. In fact, I was almost pissed off.

"*I owe you*?" I asked in disbelief. "You've got to be kidding me."

Nicholas coughed his smoker's cough. "Start with Tanaka. When I arranged your fee, over his protest mind you, well, I'm practically overlord of Tokyo. His people actually gave me a Samurai sword. But did I hear from you?"

That was it. I didn't care if he was baiting me. "As a matter of fact, you did hear from me," I yelled at him. "I sent you front row tickets to the Knicks game and a dinner reservation at Tre Salee."

"It's coming back to me now. I—"

"Save the historical revision. And you never introduced me to either Thrattas or Barpoulot. They're both from Iraklio, practically neighbors of yours. If you can't leverage me there, where the hell can you leverage me?"

"I'm working on them."

"Sure you are."

"No, I am. And you're not in Vietnam without me."

Nicholas had me there. Vietnam had been a great trip. Nicholas arranged for me to meet with the Premier in Ho Chi Min City and it led to a large contract for a software company I bankrolled that had struggled for years. Not only did it help the company grow, but it made everybody involved a lot of money.

"Okay, what the hell do you want?"

"I'll have to call you back," Nicholas said, exhaling in disgust. "My assistant is waving me to take this call. Should I try your chalet or cell phone?"

"Cell phone, assuming it's soon, like ten minutes soon. You're interrupting my morning jaunt in the hills. And not all mountain houses are chalets."

"I'll call you back shortly. I knew Vietnam would get you."

That was Nicholas, always looking for an edge. Machiavelli had his modern day incarnation in Nicholas Straka. Talk about a prince. Born into a celebrated political family in Athens renowned for their championship of the poor and a well-documented lineage to Aristotle, Nicholas had been a fair soccer player at Williams College in Massachusetts, albeit a portly one and rather slow of foot, a legendary drinker of boilermakers, and the only person in the history of Williamstown who had single-handedly devoured the thirty-six inch pepperoni monster known as *Larica's Pizza Extravaganza* in the required sixty minutes or less. The feat won him $250 and a plaque of honor on the wall. Nicholas loved that damned plaque. He loved it so much he promptly persuaded Mr. Larica to reposition it above the front door with the ruse it would increase business if seen first from the outside. Poor Mr. Larica never knew what hit him.

I first met Nicholas while a graduate student at Williams and I also never met anybody who liked him. Some of the dislike concerned superficialities: he had a sloppy appearance, his thick black hair was invariably tousled and usually unwashed, his teeth were tobacco stained even at an early age, and he had large grouper lips that dominated the lower half of his face. Even his best physical feature had a flaw; although his eyes were a handsome ocean blue, they bulged slightly from their sockets which made him seem as bloated as a puffer fish and certainly much older than his years. Never though did anyone deny his brilliance or ambition. A devout college Marxist, his heroes were Kim Philby and Guy Burgess for choosing their consciences over the privileges of class, and not once did it ever occur to him that both were traitors to their country. Nicholas had softened through the years into a democratic socialist of sorts, although I always suspected the transformation to be one of political expediency as opposed to a genuine conversion of belief, but even the Adam Smith purists on campus and firebrands of the Young Republican League admitted the genius of his mind and his invincibility in debate and both were glad to see him matriculate on schedule and finally return home to his native Greece.

Now, after years of working political connections and favors, plus a twenty year courtship of the major media and countless hours of image cultivation orchestrated by his family, Nicholas had worked himself into the position of his dreams. It seemed as Secretary General of the United Nations he might finally achieve his lifelong ambition of having his face on a stamp.

*　*　*

As promised, Nicholas called back within a few minutes.

"Hello," I said, answering the phone as I stepped through some ferns on the trail. The previous night's fog had made the ferns damp and my pants were spotted wet.

"I need you to hear me out."

I stopped walking. The weather changed with his words and although sunny outside there was an ominous darkness to the sky.

"Sure," I said, "I'll be glad to listen. You sound like your dog died. What's up?"

"Well, I'm very concerned about the Chinese posturing these past few weeks," Nicholas started, his voice deepening. "This is more than a response to GATDP, that Greater Asian Trade and Defense Pact. This is nationalism rivaling the Third Reich."

"That sounds alarmist."

"No, David, don't accuse me of being a doomster, because Xiang Chi Cheng is their Hitler. The Chinese believe the twenty first century is theirs."

"What's the driver?"

Nicholas hesitated for a moment, ruminating. "Well, to borrow from Mr. Churchill, ancient nationalism wrapped in contemporary power inside a mystery of intention," he said.

"Lots of countries conduct military exercises."

"No, it's much deeper than flexing muscle to demonstrate clout. For the first time in centuries, they are brashly dictating policy. The allusion to whatever military means are necessary was a nuclear line drawn in the sand."

"You think?"

"David, I know. Japan is the most recent power in the Far East and they've been neutered since Hiroshima and Nagasaki. The Economic Tigers, South Korea, Singapore, et al, are like Japan, economic powers without any military capabilities and are hamstrung. India is preoccupied with Pakistan. European Russia is effectively bogged down trying to Europeanize and Asiatic Russia is a joke. Even Islam has good relations with the Chinese. The only power left is America and GATDP is the modern American containment policy of George F. Kennan. The Chinese aren't standing for being hemmed in and Chinese fury knows no bounds against India. China will do everything in their power to secure continued supplies of energy."

"Sounds bad. The rumor around here is that GATDP is more military alliance than economic pact."

"It's primarily military, and the fucking Taiwanese are as intransigent as hell. Taiwan wants to sign into GATDP against Chinese wishes."

"That's a scary thought, since those antagonisms go back seventy years. China has always coveted her island neighbor. And America is treaty obligated to protect Taiwan."

I heard Nicholas sigh a troubled sigh. "It will escalate very quickly," he said, in a tone similar to a prisoner approaching the gallows. "This is worse than the Cuban Missile Crisis in 1962."

I pondered his last comment for just long enough for him to be satisfied with my pensiveness. It was also long enough for a covey of quail ahead of me to scamper across the trail.

"Well, what do you want me to do about it?" I asked.

Nicholas paused again. There was no sigh this time, but the gears in his head were grinding. I watched the quail take refuge in a thicket of sorrel not far to my right. "I'm seeking solutions anywhere I can find them," he said. "I've got friends in every country networking for answers, academics gaming every geopolitical move, diplomatic channels so fired up they're actually smoking, all working on some way out of this fucking mess. Now it's your turn."

"I'm still lost."

I heard another cough. "I need an intrepid, unconventional visionary. Everybody I've solicited is a box thinker; hell, it's like I'm sitting in a room full of crates."

"You think that's wise at a time like this?"

"I think you're brilliant."

I didn't answer him. Nicholas was patronizing me, working me, steering me toward his ends. I just waited for him to continue.

"Anyway," he said, "brilliance aside, I need your best effort. You've proven you can rake it in, now prove to me you can save the world."

I grew somewhat interested. "Well, what do you have in mind?"

"A few years back, you developed a financial plan for Global Investment Group. I know GIG and it involved billions of dollars to promote their long-term financial interests. One of the ancillary benefits coming from that study was your recommendation of an institute built around an unusual premise."

"How do you know that?"

"Howard Goldstein is a friend, on the board of GIG. So is Chip Hayward. I know the press laughed at your brainchild. Improved human relations, wasn't it?"

"Human harmony through singularity, where people think as one. Being a philanthropist as well as a venture capitalist, I want people to come together." I was still sensitive to the fact the global media and most of academia scoffed at my plan once GIG went public with my financial recommendation. "Beautiful idea, though."

"I think so too," Nicholas seconded. "I know GIG thought you were on to something. Peaceful coexistence among nations is good for business and Howard told me he believed your chosen experts could produce beneficial results. I've got half the world in economic boycotts and commerce is collapsing everywhere. You know I'm not a fan of the globalization of business, but I need strong growth rates and I need them now."

Now I sighed. The whole institute concept seemed doomed through inertia and the slowness of human minds.

"Another think tank, just what the world needs."

"There's no time for a think tank," Nicholas responded brusquely, "just do what I want."

That was the final straw. Nicholas was hiding something, something he hoped he wouldn't have to reveal. I sensed it like a cat senses a mouse.

"You're not telling me everything. Don't hold out on me, you bastard."

Nicholas groaned in resignation. Now I had him. "Can I trust you?" he pleaded with me.

"Yes."

"Are you sure?"

"Fuck yes."

I heard another sigh. "Okay, yesterday I received a letter through snail mail with a Miami postmark," he began. "The letter referenced things nobody could possibly know about me or my life. I mean impossible things: obscure governmental contacts, covert connections in the intelligence community, personal relationship details from my past, family secrets, everything. It was incredible."

"Go on."

"Well, the first paragraph proved their capabilities, the second warned me of this current crisis, and the third instructed me to contact you."

"Me?"

"Yes you. The letter also instructed me to persuade you to meet with Dr. Adrienne Stavenen."

"The professor from Berkeley? I had her pegged for my institute. She is a leading authority on solving global conflict."

"Correct. Whoever sent this letter knew that as well."

"What else did the letter mention?"

"To interview her and keep me in the loop," Nicholas said. "And your interview needs to be in person."

"What makes you say that?"

"Because the letter insisted on it."

"It did? The letter really stated that?"

"Yes David, it did. The powers behind this letter know you very well. They want you to interview Stavenen because that may save the world. You're a noted author of historical economic development and geopolitical maneuvering and you will understand her and what she has to say."

"Is that you or the letter talking?"

"Me."

I waited for two lovers on the trail to walk past me. "Assume I buy your argument," I said, rejoining my conversation with Nicholas. "Go back to Howard Goldstein. Do you think he has anything to do with the letter?"

"No, I don't."

"I agree. So who is it?"

"I don't have the foggiest."

I said nothing and waited. A hawk screeched overhead.

"David?"

"Yes, I'm still here."

Nicholas was ready to deliver his coup de grace. He was also desperate. I knew him well enough to know that if he wasn't so despairing he would have been screaming at me by now.

"You know, the world might be at stake," he eventually implored. "We might all get vaporized."

"That's pretty dramatic, even for you."

Nicholas groaned an even louder groan, this time for emphasis. "David please, I've got prophets and religious leaders proclaiming the end of the world," he shouted at me. "People are panicking. This morning, three oil tankers were sunk in the Persian Gulf and we have no idea who did it."

"Probably the Iranians," I tossed in.

"Don't count on it; Iran denies any involvement. One of my analysts thinks it's the damn Chinese."

"Well, whoever did it, oil prices will go through the ceiling."

"Yeah no shit. So David listen to me. At this precise moment in history, you are critical to our survival. The people who wrote the letter certainly think so."

Three million years of human evolution stared me in the face, replete with countless wars, genocides, environmental degradation, nuclear destructions, and a general maliciousness of men toward their fellow men. Still, something propelled humanity forward, something worth living for that I had never quite grasped, and I wanted to learn of its nature. I guess you could say it was my quest. And whoever was behind this Miami letter thought my ideas had potential.

"Well," Nicholas prodded me, "will you do it for our friendship?"

I had heard his best case. My instincts were telling me it was a giant waste of time, but someone had to be there for the petulant Greek. In fact, I was the only one outside of his family he sought in times of crisis. So there was only one thing left to do. "Fine," I blurted out, agreeing to the assignment. "But I'll need a certified letter of introduction from you sounding as official as hell. Write it yourself. It will open up doors with Stavenen, doors I couldn't open myself."

"You'll have it by tomorrow morning," Nicholas said, clapping his hands together, his phone obviously held between cheek and ear. Nothing made him happier than getting his way. "My office will set up communication procedures, as I'll be traveling the next two weeks and rarely available. Make sure you get back to me promptly."

"Is there anything else I can do for you, your majesty?"

"Only that the National Security Agency is sure to monitor us. Oh, and the letter said you may be talking to Gibson and Faro in the future; they wanted me to mention that to you as well."

"What? Seriously? I also had Gibson and Faro pegged for my institute."

Nicholas breathed in deeply. "Miami knew that, just like they know everything else; they're leading you to some result. You are being tested, for what end I really can't say."

"Nicholas, stop already. I'm in. You got your way."

I heard him hesitate for a moment. I hated it when he did that. It usually meant trouble. I wanted the conversation to end, but Nicholas clearly had more to say.

"Do you remember Dennis O'Reilly?" he asked me.

I thought for a minute. "The Williams professor caught recruiting for the CIA?"

"That's the guy. Even though we never agreed politically, he was a good man and stayed in touch with me until his death a few years back. Turns out, he was CIA to the core. Always had been. He told me something that haunted me and still does."

"Okay, I'll go along. What was it?"

Nicholas seemed to cringe. "Never repeat this," he said nervously. "Dennis said it was known within the CIA that certain operations were directed by an authority higher than the President and way past congressional oversight. He called them 'Miami,' said they were based there."

That sounded absurd. "Are you sure?"

"Hell yes, I'm sure. He said Miami had unprecedented power and could make anybody disappear. The two times Dennis had experience with them both involved potential nuclear conflicts: India against Pakistan and North Korea against South Korea."

"That seems too fantastic to believe."

"David, it's not. Dennis told me if I ever ran across Miami, the world was in grave danger. Now seems such a time. I'm scared, David, I don't want my body found in some damn dumpster."

"Nicholas, relax. I'm sure you'll be fine. I'll ask around and see what I can find."

"Don't bother, you won't learn a thing. I believe Dennis was killed because his group at the CIA uncovered Miami. He said one of his superiors wanted to investigate and was found shot in the head. Officially, the Agency blamed a Colombian drug cartel."

I remembered the case, but Nicholas was prone to histrionics and when in such moods I believed about half of what he said. "I recall that incident," I said, "the man killed was Courtney Noel and his wife was Gloria Sprague from San Francisco. The Spragues are billionaires and huge contributors to the Democrat Party; I met her once at a fundraiser in Woodside after her husband was murdered."

"David, Miami will kill anyone they have to kill. I just never want it to be me. And I wouldn't want them to kill you either."

"I will keep that in mind. Now, relax and leave it up to me."

Nicholas sighed, relieved. "Gladly, just interview Stavenen and keep me informed," he said. "And don't let me down."

I heard the phone go dead. Rarely did Nicholas say goodbye. It was a peculiar habit of his, but one I had come to accept. I glanced up the hill. On the mountain path before me, a trail snaked up a boulder strewn knoll before flattening again at the Skyward Bowl. It was a burning hike, but I loved the damn Bowl. Ground finches flitted for seeds on the roan colored, spongy ground as my thoughts scurried along with them.

Suddenly I stopped like I had been shot.

My mind was a sketch in an ancient scroll or possibly a vision from the future, some scene of pain I couldn't recognize, and in my thoughts I fell to the ground and clawed helplessly at the earth. Presciently the sensation crept into my consciousness. I sensed death and suffering. It didn't seem me, but strangely somehow was. An emptiness filled my body, an emptiness I had never known. I nearly vomited and sought the trees for answers. *What was this feeling? Why was it so terrible? Where was the feeling coming from?* I was just on a walk enjoying my morning and now I felt so miserable I trembled in my shoes.

Unhinged, I stumbled toward a nearby stream, dipping my face into a pool of crisp, clear water; the coldness of the water straightened me as I splashed more of the little brook onto my cheeks. I scanned my mind for answers. I had never experienced the scene in my thoughts. Or had I? I thought for a moment, recalling all of my time on Earth. No, I hadn't lived that scene, I was sure of it. Not even when I was young. Yet it felt so real. So what was it? Was the universe sending me a message? Was I seeing something from my future? As a child and young man, I had occasionally had portents, and although small they had certainly come true. Were they starting again? I gathered myself, splashing more water on my arms and neck. A breeze came up and calmed me. I stood up, and for the first time in minutes I breathed an effortless breath.

I searched my surroundings and saw nothing out of place.

Even the hawk was gone.

Still somewhat shaken, I breathed in the mountain air until I felt normal again. It took a few moments. I beheld the sky and the forest and my bearings steadily returned. After a time, I walked as though nothing had happened. My thoughts gradually returned to Nicholas; the fear and edginess in his voice, the seriousness of his tone, the subdued manner and careful selection in his words. Earth was indeed in trouble, the kind of trouble that can change a planet, the kind of trouble that can mean the end. I felt resolve and a sense of urgency to succeed, as I would try to do well by Nicholas and do well of myself and once again I thought of my duty and the task at hand.

TWO

Associated Press—Ashkhabad, Turkmenistan
September 3, 2017
Despite unswerving rumors of Soviet era biological weapons missing from a stockpile here in the capital city of Turkmenistan, the government of Ayad Nerrohzov categorically denied any such lapse of security. Nerrohzov himself released a document showing the lineage of biological weapons back to the fall of the Soviet regime in 1991 as consistent with both Russian and Turkmen accounting. Innuendo has suggested as many as ten biological weapons are unaccounted for by the United Nations Monitoring, Verification and Inspection Commission, UNMOVIC, and that a group of arms merchants known as Carte Blanche have them in their possession.

Eric Waller is deception. He is the most dangerous person in the world, although I use the term "person" loosely. His people, the Illick, have sought the destruction of Earth since 1945, as two atomic bomb detonations on Hiroshima and Nagasaki demonstrated to them the aggressiveness and unreasonableness of human behavior. Most galactic species avoid nuclear war with their own kind. When they don't, it sounds alarms. Earth is situated squarely in the middle of the ET4 octant of the Milky Way galaxy and the people of Earth are likely to expand in equidistant directions, increasing the likelihood of conflict with many different species in their travels, including of course the Illick.

The race known as ET4-ghal-H, humans, is a formidable species capable of splitting the atom, and in the future humans are also likely to master greater technologies like gravitational travel, electromagnetic field manipulation, fusion pulsing, and spectral density weaponry. Of more concern to the Illick is that humans have also produced "extinction event" biological weapons and continue to do so in defense laboratories flung far across their world; most of such weaponry is life threatening for all highly advanced mandrill species like the Illick, who closely resemble humans in DNA and cellular structure and are thus highly susceptible to genetically engineered viruses and antibiotic resistant bacteria. Moreover, the Illick have none of the protection afforded myself and my genus through a process known as "generational immunological satiation" which defuses even advanced biological weaponry and renders such weapons useless due to our invulnerable immune systems and psychokinetic physiology.

But there is something else at play, a hatred the Illick have for these humans that goes beyond survivability needs and proceeds rather deeply into the pathological. The Illick are possessed by a suspicion of humans that none of us in the galaxy fully comprehend, although much time and many resources have been spent evaluating the potential for warfare between these two very similar species. The Council, of which I am a member, has recently made the decision to monitor the situation without officially taking sides, but someday I hope I may understand the crux of the Illick odium for the people of this Earth.

My latest encounter with Eric Waller was in the South Bay about thirty five minutes drive from my Oakland hills home; I detest these interactions of ours, but they are vitally necessary to The Council's plans here so I do as I am instructed.

* * *

I don't know much about the town of Campbell except it's an affluent enclave and Eric was meeting with a tall, wiry man with shoulder length gray hair and a devilish black goatee. The man's eyes seemed psychotic to me. Oddly, he spoke with a muted accent, something Middle Eastern, Georgian, Armenian or possibly Turkmen. He seemed cold and impatiently precise whereas Eric is affable and engaging. I lost them in the crowded streets of shoppers, so I phoned the Campbell Inn where Eric was likely staying and checked for the alias he typically used. The clerk verified he was a guest.

I poked my head into a few of the nicer restaurants until I saw him standing at the bar of a darkened, elegant steakhouse named the Road Mill. He recognized me immediately.

"How good of you to stop by," he said sarcastically.

"Always good to see you," I replied.

There is an awkward silence as he scanned the restaurant for exits. He made a mental note and resumed.

"I don't know how you find me, but it won't do you any good," he said.

I marveled at him close up. His jaw line is so geometrically precise it seems laser cut and there are no visible features belying his race. My eyes in direct sunlight are difficult to explain, although my golden sparkles have been explicated as a slight genetic anomaly and my other giveaway, an extra bone at the temple, is only discernable to evolutionary biologists and max-illofacial surgeons; but Eric is so uncannily human it defies explanation.

"So what are you doing in Campbell?" I finally ask him.

Eric Waller's geometry becomes more exact. "You stalk me like some crazed jilted lover. Tragic really, but that's what I expect from you."

"Just doing my job."

"So what do you want this time?"

"Nothing I haven't wanted before. Who was the goateed creep I saw you with earlier?"

"Sorry, you're wasting your time. And remember the treaty; I am *desalgen*. My murder leads to galactic war."

That was a true statement, the Illick having expressed a willingness to wage total war if any of their desalgen were ever harmed (desalgen is the Illick word for meritorious royalty). Although The Council would win such a war as well, the costs would be appalling, setting all combatants back centuries or even millennia.

"I don't want to kill you," I said, "I just want you to reconsider your mission."

His black eyes stared into mine. "I'm vacationing, don't you find this town a veritable resort?"

I laughed at him. "Humans may yet turn themselves around," I suggested. "Why don't you give them a chance?"

Whatever jovialness Eric possessed quickly dissipated. "They choose violence. They're an inferior species, threatening us all. Even your superiors should recognize that."

"Yes, but human shortcomings are counterbalanced by their emerging spirituality, artistic sensibilities, business acumen, technological development, scientific progress, and now environmentally sustainable worldviews. And the Illick have fought many wars."

"Only when forced to defend ourselves."

I shot him a look of disdain. "That's bullshit," I retorted. "Illick civilization is ten times more likely to wage war than any other culture in the galaxy."

"Everyone is jealous of us, what can I say?"

It was hard to keep my cool. "Jealous?" I roared. "You're racial supremacists. Here they're called Nazis. Do you know how many societies you've subjugated and slaughtered? No one is jealous, we're righteous."

"Righteous?" Eric shouted back, scowling. "Is it righteous to colonize the galaxy while our alliances were overrun? Is it righteous to confine us? How about the millions of Illick slaughtered by your armies?"

"Brought on by your expansionism. We lost millions more."

"We will not be contained."

"But The Council prevailed in every case."

I saw a look of condescension. "Things are changing. You will live just long enough to witness our invincibility and then I will kill you."

"You may try to kill me. You have been trying for years and I am still here."

Eric laughed at me. "Oh, I *will* kill you," he said, savoring the thought. "But you will suffer the insufferable first. Then your alliances will burn in the fires of our *legentcras*." Legentcras is the Illick word for 'extermination centers.' The Illick have murdered millions on occupied planets and planned to murder hundreds of millions more before The Council intervened. He twisted away and walked toward the exit.

I couldn't stop him. The treaty stipulates the Illick have free rein on Earth as long as they keep their identity secret and send no more than five members of their race here at once. The Council attempts to monitor the number, but there could be more than we suspect. Eric turned to face me as he left the restaurant and laughed another cocky laugh. He held up both hands outstretched to indicate the number ten with his fingers.

"Ten is a better number than five, don't you think?"

I got the message. Ten Illick were on Earth.

He spun again and walked away.

There was nothing I could do.

THREE

Reuters—Beijing, China
September 4, 2017

The government of China today announced its intention to conduct a naval blockade of Taiwan if the Taiwanese government becomes a signatory to the recent GATDP agreement between the United States and several Asian nations including India, Japan, and South Korea. The United States swiftly condemned the announcement and countered that any such naval blockade will be considered an act of war, triggering the United States' obligation to defend Taiwan against forcible reunification.

Jenny Scott Wright was once the Carl Sandburg poetry winner at the University of San Francisco, the first year the literature department offered the prize, the same year her mother Carol Scott was diagnosed with aggressive breast cancer and had to quit her job. That was eight years ago and Jenny told me Carol fought the disease as courageously as anyone at the Cancer Clinic ever remembered seeing, for nearly a full seven of those years. Her father, Albert Wright, died when Jenny was just a toddler, although her two best friends, Trisha and Sharon, recently told me that Jenny kept a picture of her father with her in a locket worn loosely around her neck. Only after last year when Carol died did Jenny put the locket in a drawer to honor one of her mother's final requests; seems Carol didn't want Jenny weighted down for another moment by any kind of loss, no matter how distant in years or how light a locket lays on a young woman's chest. Jenny's autumn moon eyes still get teary when we talk about Carol so I try to avoid the subject. Still, it comes up now and again and Jenny clutches my hand with hers and I feel the shakiness in her touch as she looks away and remembers her mom.

I first met Jenny when she interviewed me for the San Francisco Chronicle's Business Section while researching a story on globalization and its deleterious effects on the global underclass. Jenny cares intensely about the poor. She also cares loads for animals, spending the first ten minutes of my interview telling me about her latest adoption of a stray chocolate and white tabby she found crying near the city trash heap one particularly cold and foggy night, now known famously as Sammy the Brown.

Jenny's favorite restaurant is the Amanda Street Bistro, jutting off the steepest slope of San Francisco's legendary Russian Hill; she clumsily burst through the front door, slowed her steps, and exhaled the day's aggravation. Her eyes searched for me inside the darkness of the room. Dressed in a tight fitting black skirt and a checkerboard red and black sweater, she looked like a vintage Ferrari on display. She walked toward me and placed her purse on the bar.

"How's the Brown," I asked her.

"We need to work on that," Jenny said, her smile quickly forming a frown. "Hug me before you do anything else."

I stood up from my seat at the bar and gave her a hug. She smelled wonderfully of tropical berries.

"That better?" I asked her, pulling away.

"Much. And the Brown got sick on my carpet this morning, thank you kindly. Want a cat?"

"Want a drink?"

Jenny reached into her purse. "Sure, peach cosmopolitan," she said, fumbling for something. She pulled out her lipstick. "Aren't you starving?"

"I've been hungrier. Anniversaries make me nervous."

Jenny smirked. "You think you're nervous now, just wait," she said, curling the lipstick around her lips. "The word of the day is commitment."

I gulped hard.

Jenny cocked her head and pleaded into my eyes. "You're fifteen years my senior, graying on the sides, and I had to ask you out. I'm saving you from a life alone."

"Very kind of you."

"And why aren't you fretting?"

"What? I am fretting. Sounds like we might be going exclusive."

"No, we're already exclusive, but the world is imploding and you've barely said a word. Some evangelical today called for internment camps for Chinese Americans."

"No? He actually called for internment camps?"

"Yes, and now the Ukrainian water supply has been poisoned by the Russians. At least that's what the BBC reported."

"The Ukrainians have been using China as a wedge against Russia," I noted. "So that makes sense. But the BBC has been off lately in their reporting. And wow, I guess we're exclusive."

"You should be frightened for society right now," Jenny said, ignoring me, her eyes drawn and troubled. "My editorial board thinks we're headed to World War III. And these are some of the most informed people in the country."

"Who says I'm not worried?"

I saw another frown. "No, you should *feel* the crisis. That's what I'm saying—you don't feel."

"I feel something."

Jenny was Lee at Appomattox. It wasn't as much defeat as it was inevitability.

"I want you to feel more deeply; for society, for poor people, for animals, and mostly for me. See, it hurts when you don't feel as much as I do because I've fallen in love with you," she said tenderly, her hand dampening as it held my own. "I love you so much."

Somewhere, somewhere deep inside of me, I felt a ball of happiness rising from the tension in my stomach. It was the first time anyone had ever said they loved me.

Moments passed where little else happened except my beaming. We took a nearby table and sat down.

Finally Jenny spoke. "Well, at least you're not angry with me."

I didn't want the feeling of happiness to end, but I had to say something. "Have I told you how marvelous you are? You're the most incredible woman I've ever met, the grandest adventure I could ever imagine."

"Really?"

"Yes, absolutely, every moment is an escapade. You make me so happy."

This time, Jenny rubbed my arm with both hands. Her touch was so soft, so nice to feel, I had to pull away just to survive it.

"Do you know you have the most beautiful eyes I've ever seen," she said, beholding me. "Your eyes have tiny flecks of gold like little amber sequins, each one so shiny and bright. Where did you get such beautiful eyes?"

Such talk always troubled me. My eyes were a clue to my race. "Genetics is all I can say," I eventually responded. "It's nothing I can take credit for."

Jenny hugged my feet with hers under the table. Her face seemed as an angel. "I want you to love me. It's my dream. I have waited all my life for you."

I tried to find the words, but they weren't there. I felt myself fidgeting.

"Can't say the words?" Jenny asked.

Abland Pargenni, the Omani economic minister and a friend of mine from years past, once told me shortly after his wife passed away that humans are at their best when things are at their worst. I saw it in Jenny just then. She never pulled away or changed her look of love.

"It's okay," she said, as softly as a moment prior, "someday you will love me. I will just keep trying and one day I will break through."

I stared into Jenny's eyes. "I'd like that as well. It's just—well, how do I say this, I'm still learning what love is. And I have been warned not to love."

That was a slip on my part. Jenny caught it.

"Warned by whom?"

"Let's just say by those who don't think I'll handle it well. But I want to learn of love."

The deflection worked. "I have a confession to make," Jenny said. "I haven't been myself ever since I knew I'd fallen in love with you. I have tried to protect myself, and I guess I'm frustrated that I can't stop my feelings for you. Yesterday, I snapped at Marlene Lowell and today I accused Topeka Tom, my favorite cabbie in the whole world, of deliberately taking side roads to up his fare. And I trashed you tonight when we first greeted each other. But I didn't see the connection between my worrying if you loved me and my general state of irritation. Now I do."

Jenny started to stand up from the table.

"Where are you going?" I asked, grabbing her arm.

"I need to go look in the mirror and ask myself why I've been so boorish."

"But wait. I don't think you're boorish. I think you're wonderful."

Jenny stopped in her tracks. She gazed afar and her eyes got moist.

"My mother used to say I was wonderful. And now you said it. Hold that thought and I will be back in a bit."

* * *

As fate would have it, while Jenny was in the restroom I received a call from Christopher Thrattas, one of the Greeks from Athens I had asked Nicholas to engage so that another investment group I represent could gain entrée into the security systems markets in Greece.

"This is David Jordan," I answered.

"Good afternoon, this is Christopher Thrattas, former head of the EYP, the Greek Intelligence Service, and I understand you're a friend of Nicholas Straka. The business he stated is not the reason for my call. I am hoping you might do me a favor."

"I'm in a restaurant, let me step outside."

I found the back balcony. The view was spectacular. Sloops and yawls sliced the copper bay, while seagulls glinted through cottony mists. I almost forgot I was on a phone call. "Can you hear me?" I finally asked him.

"Yes, perfectly."

"So, what can I do for you?"

"Do you know Admiral Thompson's theory on Carte Blanche?" Thrattas asked me.

Admiral Thompson was the Deputy Director of the NSA. He was a brilliant man, but somewhat controversial. "Sure, I know his theory," I responded. "Carte Blanche is a group of arms dealers based in Turkmenistan and Thompson said they're the group most likely to possess weapons from the old Soviet arsenal."

"You have a good security clearance. Don't ask me how I know that."

"Nicholas can't keep a secret," I said, smelling a rat.

I heard a laugh. "Oh, there are other ways to know of you, Mr. Jordan. You will learn those in time."

I disregarded his comment. I knew the EYP probably had their methods. "Well, I know Carte Blanche is shadowy," I said. "Thompson believes they stole weapons with a Soviet general's complicity sometime in the early nineties."

"Thompson is correct. The bio-weapons in question are considered near extinction devices. It appears the government of Turkmenistan provides protection for the cartel."

"Why would Turkmenistan do that?"

"Turkmenistan is held hostage by the threat of the weapons being used against them."

"Has Carte Blanche transacted with anyone?"

"Yes."

"What nation?"

"We're not sure it's a nation."

"Great, that could be anybody then. So what's the favor?"

"Nicholas said you're on special assignment for him, so succeed Mr. Jordan. That's my favor. You must prove your worth. The biological weapons club is growing and this crisis creates a highly unstable environment. Anything could happen."

"Mr. Thrattas, I understand, but prove my worth to whom?"

"You will learn that in time as well. The security business you seek is more intricate than you could imagine. For now, all I can give you is some backdrop."

That was disappointing, but I can tell when someone will not budge from their position. "All right, tell me what you know," I said.

"Well, the Chinese have withdrawn their ambassador to India and have ceased diplomatic relations with South Korea. They have sold advanced missile technology to Pakistan and are assisting the Pakistani army along the Kashmiri border against the Indians. Their actions are designed to punish India for her participation in GATDP."

"Kashmir's incendiary," I noted.

"The place most likely to cause World War III."

"Do you think the Chinese will attack India through Pakistan?"

"Eventually, yes. We suppose the Chinese will destroy the Srisailam, Bhakra, and Hirakud Dams. This will incapacitate India."

I was shocked. "Millions of people will starve as India loses her power grid," I remarked.

"Now you're catching on."

I knew that India was sure to retaliate, probably with nuclear weapons. "Is there anything else?" I asked.

"Get to Dr. Adrienne Stavenen. She is critical to your mission and your development. And plan on visiting Miami."

"Miami?"

"Yes, the city in Florida. If you're successful, you will learn the secrets of the world."

"Secrets, what secrets? What the hell are you talking about?"

"Goodbye Mr. Jordan. Dr. Stavenen is the first step. Remember this conversation."

I heard the phone call disconnect. His last few comments to me were particularly odd. None of them made any sense, but it felt like I was being tested. Moreover, he sounded unusually connected, like someone privy to information reserved for heads of state. The air felt suddenly cold. I started back toward the restaurant to order dinner, wondering about Thrattas and who he represented, but by then Jenny was at the balcony and opened the door for me.

"Everything okay?" she asked me.

"Nothing is ever okay. But now I'm starving, so let's eat."

* * *

After dinner Jenny and I hailed a town car from an Indonesian émigré named Kediri and he dropped us off for a nightcap at Laguna Street Café. We sat by a popping fireplace and ordered. The waiter soon brought us two cognacs and a bottle of flavored water.

"This ought to help," he said.

"Help with what?" I asked him.

The waiter looked at both Jenny and I, a little embarrassed. "I'm sorry sir, just everyone tonight, well......we get lots of financial district types and the market—"

"Oh yes, I turned it off when the Dow was down a thousand," I said, quickly realizing I interrupted him. Jenny gave me a look. "Did it get any worse?"

"Yes sir, down fifteen hundred. They expect more shorting tomorrow. Damn global crisis, killing business."

The three of us commiserated in our glances and the waiter went to serve another table.

Jenny had something to say and she said it after the first sip of cognac warmed her stomach. "I also have a bit of news. Michel promoted me to business correspondent today."

"Fantastic. What incredible thing did you do to deserve a promotion?"

"Well, my boyfriend is a board director of my parent company. I think that had something to do with it."

"I exerted no influence."

"Sure."

"No, I mean it. I had nothing to do with your promotion."

I took my first drink of flavored water. Both cognacs were for Jenny. I knew she'd want a second cognac and since she never likes to wait for drinks I ordered the second with the first.

"Well, how about that," she eventually said, immersed in the miracle of her own achievement. "I climbed the corporate ladder on my own. Probably didn't hurt I'm sleeping with the publisher."

"You're what?"

Jenny batted her eyelashes, her eyes sparkling with glee. "Oh, so you're jealous?" she asked me, knowing the answer. "That's very close to love. You should be more careful."

She had me, what could I do. "Okay, fine, but I see how that old geezer ogles you," I replied. "I should smack him, but I'd rather not ruin a perfectly good fossil."

"Don't you dare smack him or say a thing. I need this job. And he's not a geezer; he's only five years older than you. Anyway, my first assignment is in China, which is a tough fold of the map these days."

"You're not traveling to China. I forbid it. Are you insane?"

"Oh, stop it, I have to go. The hottest story in China is Mien Jinkao, the democratic reformer from Hangzhou whose expatriate daughter Tietnan lives here in San Francisco. Tietnan and I have become friends."

"I know of Mien Jinkao. What's her daughter like?"

"Well, she is very bright and plenty informed. Sharon and I had drinks with Tietnan at Boulevard last week and Tietnan is writing Mien on my behalf. I am going to have a conversation with her."

I had to change the subject before Jenny asked me to visit China with her; I knew I wouldn't have the time, although it would have been nice to go. "Say, did you know Nicholas Straka is a friend of mine?"

Jenny put her hand to her mouth. "Cod face? The Secretary General of the United Nations?"

"Yes him."

Jenny looked a bit sheepish. "Forgive me, that's mean, but he does resemble a giant sea bass and he's a notoriously ruthless scumbag from a billionaire family in Greece."

"Yes, he's plenty rich."

"And he cheats on his wife with a gorgeous Hungarian actress."

"She's not much of an actress."

Jenny looked disapprovingly confounded. "Why didn't you tell me you're pals with Straka?"

"I didn't know you'd be impressed."

Jenny took a big sip of cognac, more like a full swallow. "So go on, tell me more," she said. "I still can't believe you know the guy. He is front and center right now."

"Well, Nicholas is distraught over the GATDP agreement and the Chinese reaction to the pact. He doesn't want the world blowing up on his watch, so he solicited my services."

Jenny nearly dropped her glass. "What the hell can you do?" she asked incredulously. "I mean, I love you and all, but you're one man."

She had a point, even if she was wrong about my lineage. "Well first up, I'm meeting with Dr. Adrienne Stavenen, the famous historian and economist from Berkeley who advises the IMF and World Bank. She won't talk to Nicholas because of some chicanery years ago, but she is a great resource."

"I think I've heard the name. Why talk to her?"

"Well, for one, she's an expert on building human harmony. She wrote the definitive paper on globalization and mass consensus. And secondly, some furtive group wants me to meet with her as well; they told Nicholas as much. Somebody thinks I can do something."

"You mean the CIA?"

I shouldn't have brought Miami up in our conversation. "No, I'm not sure of their identity, but I'll figure it out," I answered. "Hell, maybe it is the CIA."

Jenny ruminated for a moment. "Well, be careful, those guys are dangerous. Is there anybody else you'll be seeing?"

"I may also speak with Robert Allen Gibson and Manuela Faro. The former is the most eminent physicist and security expert on Earth and the latter is probably the smartest person in human history. Both could be very valuable right now."

"Over my dead body you will meet Faro. She is gorgeous. Glamour recently proclaimed her the most beautiful face in history. I don't want you anywhere near that woman."

I had to laugh. "Now who's jealous?" I asked.

There was an odd silence. It seemed as though Jenny reconciled something in her mind. "Okay, you can meet Faro, but don't sit too close. I hear she has magical charms."

"I would never cheat on you."

"You better not if you want to live. But isn't Faro a philosopher of technology or some other esoteric thing? How is she going to help stop a growing international calamity?"

"She is consulted on virtually everything, from environmental disasters to economic trends to security issues to space exploration. Her work on international relations is unsurpassed. Once, she even authored a secret study identifying cities most likely to be nuclear targets; I perused it for an investment prospectus I did."

"Global conglomerates actually plot which cities might get nuked?"

"Sad, isn't it? Faro's technological expertise and philosophical logic in that study was extraordinary. Keep this quiet, but she's a paid consultant on many NATO projects, as I'm sure is Gibson."

"I knew Faro had few peers, but I didn't know she was immersed in global security issues. She must be working overtime in this crisis."

"I'm sure she is."

"Well, she better bring her best game if she is dealing with China. I mean, working with that government is like pushing on a string."

I gazed into the fire. Glasses clinked behind and to the sides of me. The air was warm and seemed to coax me with a relaxing assuredness. It was time for an admission.

"I must be successful in stopping this escalating global crisis. If the conflict turns intractably toward war and the nuclear option is utilized, there will be dire consequences. Horrors you can't imagine."

"Oh, I've seen pictures of Hiroshima and Nagasaki. I know full well what—."

"No, not that, there are far worse things than mushroom clouds."

Jenny looked at me like I was an idiot. "What's worse than nuclear annihilation?" she asked.

I doubt I would have continued with my explanation had I not cared so much for the woman in front of me. My affection and trust in her was somehow superseding my directives. That was dangerous.

"Acculturation," I finally said. "The loss of a culture's identity and what it thinks of itself. That can never be regained after a nuclear war."

"You mean after a nuclear war people will never again look at themselves quite the same way? Maybe like how Germans were never the same after The Holocaust?"

It seemed a good out. Not the truth, but a good out. "Yes, something along those lines," I said, as convincingly as I could. I remained quiet again as the fire continued to pop.

Jenny drew melancholy. "Why do we always fight wars, anyway?" she asked, watching the fire pop along with me. "What the hell is the matter with people?"

Red flags were popping up all around me, going off in my head like alarms. Still, I continued to reveal more than I should have. "Have you heard of the Triune Brain?" I asked her.

"No, what's that?"

"It's simple, really. Humans have three basic components comprising their brain: a reptilian base; a mammalian section covering the base; and a neo-mammalian overlay which provides people with their higher order intelligence. Each is its own layer and each higher layer is more advanced than the one below it."

"Oh wait, I do know about the Triune Brain, it's very interesting, read about it in an anthropology class years ago."

"Yes, but no one here knows the exact working relationship between all three layers or how they interface and share function together."

Jenny seemed bothered. "Are you saying human harmony and our brains are somehow connected?" she asked.

"That's exactly what I'm saying, but the better way to view the connection is that the human brain is disharmonious by its very nature. Humans fight wars because the human brain is insufficiently evolved."

"So what's the hope?"

This was risky territory because it hinted at my genotype, but I couldn't stop myself. "In time, humans will evolve a fourth lobe," I started, gauging Jenny's reaction. "This fourth lobe will act as a super-coordinator of the other three and provide an incredible level of rationality people have been lacking."

Jenny smiled at me. "I get it," she said, "if humans don't kill themselves off, evolution takes us to that fourth lobe. Then we'll be too smart to make ourselves extinct. Is that right?"

"Evolution or genetic engineering, it can be either."

"No? You're not saying—"

"Yes, there is ongoing work expanding cranial capacity and artificially creating a fourth lobe through cybernetics. One lab in Asia is within a few decades of trials."

"Come on David, you're joking?"

"No, their managers feel they're close to a breakthrough. So GATDP and the Chinese reaction have gotten everyone at these labs extremely nervous. Governments across the world have task forces, kept secret of course, studying whether humans will perservere. Remember, most species don't survive."

Jenny cringed at the thought. "That's a bleak outlook, even if Charles Darwin would agree," she said, massaging her shoulder. Massaging was a habit of hers when she was worried. "People deserve more, David, so I'm glad you're doing your part."

"Yes, but from a cosmological perspective, it's actually more important the planet endures. Species come and go, but planets capable of sustaining life are the jewels of the galaxy and must be protected at all costs."

"And so any event leading to a furthering of war increases our chance of extinction?"

"No doubt. Just think about it; humans may be only decades away from building lasting peace and here they are with their fingers on the launch buttons."

Jenny rolled her eyes, let out a deep breath, and shook her head again in disgust. "Nicholas Straka," she stated disapprovingly.

"What about him?"

"You'll be helping a rat."

"Rats are animals too."

Jenny came forward and lifted her chin smugly. She seemed resigned to the fact I'd be joining forces with a man half the world hated. Still, when she got like this, where she thought she had me, she sparkled like a firework.

"You're beginning to like animals as much as I do. Rats, cats, what's the difference, right?"

"I suppose so."

"Good, Carole Ann Carver today at work passed around a flyer of the cutest kitty cat you ever saw and he desperately needs a home."

"Oh no," I said, extending my arms in the classic defensive gesture. "You tricked me. You're not playing fair."

I felt Jenny's foot under the table rub against my leg, first up and down my calf and then onto my ankle. "I never play fair," she said, her eyes dripping honey. "You should know that after all these months together."

"Where's that check?" I yelled impatiently, looking around for the waiter, recalling when Jenny and I are alone.

Jenny burst out laughing. The waiter came over with the tab in hand. "Here you are, sir," he said. "Is there anything else I can do for you?"

"Not a thing," I said hastily. I left a fifty and together Jenny and I climbed into a waiting taxi hugging Jackson Street, the mist thickening into a blurring fog.

"Cow Hollow," I told the cab driver, "Chestnut and Fillmore."

"Yes sir," the cabbie answered.

"You were saying something about a primitive brain?" Jenny whispered to me mischievously, leaning on my shoulder in the back seat as the cab sped away.

I gazed down at her. The city lights reflected well into the backseat, alternately brightening Jenny's face and then shadowing it, the effect accentuating her delicate features and highlighting her wondrously thick hair. She was so pretty in the changing patina I had to kiss her. "Hell, I'm a male,"

I finally mustered, whispering softer than Jenny had whispered to me, "I could have nine lobes in my brain and it wouldn't help me when you start being sexy."

Jenny put on some more lipstick and smacked her lips together. "Men, you're all the same," she said, rubbing my legs slowly near my thighs with her hands. "About as complex as a bread crumb. I own you, admit it."

There was nothing I could say. I just squirmed. Soon, we were back at her apartment and when the curtains were drawn my memory had served me well.

FOUR

Associated Press—New Delhi, India
September 5, 2017

The government here today announced a military alert for its western provinces of Gujarat, Rajasthan, Punjab and Kashmir after skirmishes erupted between Indian and Pakistani forces along the Kashmiri border. According to defense officials who requested anonymity, full military alerts for the northern provinces of Arunachal Pradesh and Himalchal Pradesh along the Chinese border will soon follow.

In my study at home the following night, I awaited confirmation from Dr. Stavenen. Nicholas had dutifully sent me the letter of introduction I requested in an official e-mail from the United Nations and I had forwarded it on to her. I was about to read an article she wrote regarding historical patterns of war when I heard a forceful knocking on my front door.

Peering through the glass was Donald Niebauer, dressed in his usual gray sweater and khaki slacks, an associate for a number of years and one of my kind, holding a large black device obviously weighing a great deal and threatening to slip from his arms. Hurriedly, I opened the front door. Donald's face bulged red from the strain of carrying the object and he quickly made his way through my entryway and into the study where he sat the box-shaped device down on a cabinet cap. He exhaled forcefully after setting down the contraption.

"One hundred and twenty pounds," he said, catching his breath. "Not an ounce lighter."

"It won't damage the wood, I hope. You should have called first."

"No time for a call. Ambassador Wren is none too pleased."

"Oh really, why's that?"

Donald straightened his back. "Because you're not embedded," he said, his tone rising. "That's the word The Ambassador used."

I was in no mood. "Embedded? Are you kidding me? I'm a fucking tick. You two need to relax; I'll have a recommendation within a month."

"This rotten apple won't make it another month. The Kashmiri conflict is escalating. If The Council has to intervene, you get a one way ticket out of here."

That was the price of my failure. Ambassador Wren had in no uncertain terms told me I would be reassigned if an intervention proved necessary. I would also be demoted, with limited travel privileges.

"Has The Council increased aerial surveillance?" I asked. "Humans notice our craft when we flit in and out of their clouds. Their UFO sites and blogosphere are lighting up like Christmas trees."

"We have doubled our efforts, and if this crisis escalates, we will double again. We are clustering over certain war fronts and nuclear launch facilities to signal our concern; hopefully, these dimwits will figure it out."

"Are our emissaries materializing at their secret bases?"

Donald groaned. "No, The Council recently discontinued that program because of discussions at Area 51. Our assessment is that humans are becoming more territorial."

I scoffed at him. "It is their planet you know," I added. "The Council should have anticipated that behavior."

"Well, it may not be their planet much longer. Our observations show the Pakistanis are flying fighter sorties and short range bomber runs into Kashmir, assisted by China and Iran. They are causing lots of damage. Pakistan and India have nukes."

"I know."

"Well, did you know Chinese troops have massed along the Tibetan and Nepalese borders?"

"Yes, preparing to invade India."

Donald's face tensed. He glanced away in disgust, gradually returning his eyes to mine. "Straka is fraying," he said, "and this dump of a rock is about to implode. If that happens, say goodbye to your girlfriend."

I wanted to punch him. In his early sixties here, it wouldn't have been much of a fight. He had rolled his sweater sleeves up during our conversation; his forearms, chalky white and freckled, still shook from the strain of carrying the heavy device. He noticed I noticed the trembling in his arms.

"Been drinking again?" I asked him. Beads of sweat suddenly appeared on his forehead.

"A beer now and then. But only when I get home from work."

"Yeah sure. You know the damage alcohol does to our systems. But hell, I won't pass that little tidbit along to Ambassador Wren."

"You promise?"

I snickered at Donald's cowardice. He was a slave to Ambassador Wren. "Yeah, I promise," I finally said. "Now what the hell is this device?"

"It's the new uploading equipment," Donald said, rather proudly. "And thanks. You and I go back a long way and I apologize for being short with you."

Peace made, I was again reminded of my duty. I stared at the contraption that seemed destined to dent my fine cabinetry. "Okay, so what does this thing do again?"

"It's your new communication device with The Council, named after Edward Wassler at RSG Corporation, as he was one of our best agents. He was summoned home before we finished the prototype."

"Oh yes, I remember Wassler. His tolerance for the atmosphere here was especially low, causing rapid brain degeneration in just a year or two. Good guy though. So how do I operate this hunk of bolts?"

Donald pressed a shiny gold button the size of a quarter on the front of the device. A flat platform slid out from near the bottom. "Type your report here," he said, pointing to the platform. "Gently touch the big blue knob on top when the transmission is complete and return the switches to their starting positions. Never violate the sequence."

"Why?"

"The machine generates a small gravity field that might expand beyond the room. Somebody discovers that and we've got some explaining to do."

"Simple. Anything else I should know?"

"To operate the machine remotely you just need an Internet connection."

I almost spit my gum out. "Come on Donald, the Internet? What the hell? We might as well use smoke signals."

"Make fun if you must, but our encryption keeps us hidden and using their Internet is cost effective. We thought of a proprietary system, but emissions were traceable."

Actually, that made good sense. Ambassador Wren was a stickler for stealth and cost control. "Okay, can we talk briefly about the BMS system before you leave?" I asked.

The BMS or Biological Monitoring Scan is the name of the nano-technology device implanted into Eric Waller's brain by The Council. It's a truly marvelous technology made of organic material and heuristic computer modeling far ahead of anything the Illick possess; its primary limitation is that it can't be used continuously.

"Are you seeing the world through Eric Waller's eyes?" Donald asked. "The BMS is supposed to do that for you."

"Yes, that's how I found him in Campbell. He suspects we're monitoring him. I wish I knew his thoughts."

"Sorry, the system is not there yet. But we're working on it. Oh, and you can use it remotely through a laptop or smart phone."

"I have already been doing that. But why can I use the BMS for only an hour or so every couple of days?"

Donald stepped back defensively. "Well," he said, "the scatter optics retrieves his field of vision and generates three dimensional milieus so you're in the room with him. Have you seen that?"

"Yes. But you didn't answer my question."

Donald had the same look as a criminal realizing he was caught on video. He wouldn't make eye contact with me. "Waller is tracked through GPS and photo-imaged into our heuristic computer for an assessment of his intentions given his surroundings."

I lost my patience. "Okay, you're not answering my question because....."

Donald winced. He stared at the ground. "The BMS may not work forever," he said, "in fact, it may—"

"For the love of God, don't tell me that, Donald," I shouted, a mission commander when the rocket fails. "I must have the BMS. It has to work. Do you understand me?"

Donald began to shake again. He looked down. I felt myself slumping. "Sorry," Donald said weakly, without looking up. "I thought we would have made the improvements by now......."

"Eric Waller is launching a plot," I responded despairingly, trying to rouse him. "These are Illick we're talking about; they don't get any more dangerous."

"We're trying our best."

"Donald, I need that BMS. It fails and we fail."

"Ambassador Wren said you'll figure something out. He seemed almost confident."

I was a defendant hearing a guilty verdict. Next came the sentencing. "You have more bad news for me, don't you?" I asked him, anticipating the worst. "Come on, out with it."

Donald continued staring at the floor. When his face rose up again, his eyes looked like punctured balloons.

"There's been another amendment to the treaty," he said.

"What? No way, again? What the hell this time? How many damn amendments are we going to make?"

Donald recoiled in anticipation that I might explode. "The amendment stipulates the Illick must remain covert and cannot attack Earth directly," he said meekly. "But if humans enter an extinction war with themselves, The Council won't interfere as long as the planet is preserved."

"Was anybody going to tell me about this amendment?"

"Ambassador Wren thought you'd be upset."

"Upset? Yeah, I'm upset. The Illick want humans to self-destruct. They may get their way. So The Council doesn't think human life is worth preserving?"

"Not exactly, but humans are on trial."

I breathed in deeply. This treaty amendment was particularly bad news. I knew The Council would take every step to preserve the planet, but it was apparent they considered humans expendable. That thought triggered another. "So Eric's plot must kill off humans and yet preserve the biosphere?" I asked rhetorically, studying the room.

Donald being Donald, he answered anyway. "That seems logical," he said.

I glanced at him. "And this crisis shouldn't lead to nuclear war, at least not fully?"

"No, we will launch CX."

CX is the positioning of global overlay stations in space to conduct the intervention necessary to save a planet from itself. Once in place, it can intercept all nuclear missiles and dropped atomic bombs. It's a more active phase than observation, although still reversible without consequence. Innocence can be preserved in CX, but never in actual intervention. In an intervention, the resident civilization must comply with a number of measures necessary to safeguard the planet; this causes a 'crisis of self' where the indigenous peoples are forced to accept their subordinate position. In almost every case, the results of CX are traumatic.

"CX isn't perfect," I said, rejoining the conversation. "There have been mistakes."

Donald sensed my urgency. "You're thinking of Stakigue 9?"

"Yes, CX malfunctioned and the planet was lost."

Donald nodded acknowledgement. "But CX has a lifetime positive outcome ratio of 97:1 and enhancements are being made all the time," he said.

"Tell that to the Staks."

I walked Donald out of my study and into the entry foyer, past sentinel paintings of Lincoln and Wilson perched above large marble stands brought over from Crete. Donald seemed oblivious to great leaders of men and cared little for human culture. Neither did he notice the Etruscan tile on which he stood. I should have liked Donald, but I cared for many humans more, even Nicholas and the men who worship at the altar of glory.

"You will be successful, won't you?" Donald asked, stepping into the center of the foyer. "Ambassador Wren said you might be having visions, insights into the future, as a gift from The One. You had some in your youth. Are you having any revelations that might help us?"

I thought back to the terror in the forest after my conversation with Nicholas. "Perhaps, but none that I can see helping us," I said. "The only vision I've had was dark and devoid of hope."

Donald perked up. "Ambassador Wren wanted me to assure you to welcome them all," he said. "Maybe your visualizations are a premonition of Earth's future?"

"Well, I sure as hell hope not. There's not much future in that."

Donald found another thought. "It could be too that your system is becoming intolerant to the conditions of Earth, mimicking mental disease," he said. "You have been here for decades. So keep us informed. Humans are burning their cities and crying for blood. Soon, the rioting will turn to slaughter."

"I'll do my best. But I need that BMS to work. So keep working on improvements."

Donald turned and faced my direction. He said nothing. The light from the hanging chandelier shone directly in his eyes. As he lifted his head the light caught him at a definitive angle; his eyes shone the unmistakable golden flecks of my very own eyes. I felt familiarity as Donald made his way to his car. He was unavoidably mine. The engine was still running from his arrival and he drove off without saying another word to me. I closed the large oaken door behind me, ever so thankful for his pithy goodbye.

* * *

Shortly after Donald's visit I received a confirmation e-mail from Dr. Adrienne Stavenen, wishing to see me the following day. The escalating global crisis was consuming not only the airwaves, but the calendars of those deemed in any way luminaries to the unfolding world events; Dr. Stavenen had just returned from Washington where she had briefed the Senate Foreign Relations Committee on Sino-American relations and the likelihood of war resulting from GATDP and the current crisis. Fortunately, she worked only a short drive away on the University of California campus, easily accessible for me through the back roads of Grizzly Peak and Strawberry Canyon.

At that moment, the land line rang and I answered, hearing the remote static of an international call.

"Is this David Jordan?" a feminine voice asked me.

"Yes, speaking."

"This is Manuela Faro. I know of you and your work."

I was plenty surprised, as I had never met the woman. "How do you know of me?"

"You come highly recommended from Bradley Manning."

"Okay, so how do you know Brad?"

"Come now, Mr. Jordan, who doesn't?"

She had me there. Bradley Manning was CEO of Innovative Systems Corporation and an icon of Silicon Valley. He was an influential leader in global business as well as a benefactor of the United Nations. He knew everyone and everyone knew him.

"For what it's worth, Bradley said you're a crack venture capitalist and a fair libertarian," Manuela Faro went on. "He said I could count on you."

"That was nice of him. Count on me for what?"

I was ignored. "Now how the crap do you know Nicholas Straka?" she asked. "That's a hell of a man to know at a time like this."

"Nicholas and I went to school together at Williams College in Massachusetts. He's not as bad as they say."

"Oh, I don't hold anything against him. I know Washington thinks he's a disgusting louse threatening American hegemony, but I adore the fact he's a rash for conservatives."

"That he is. I'd say conservatives dislike him as much as they dislike anybody."

There was a pause. I wondered if I had lost the call. "Mr. Jordan, have you ever thought of visiting Argentina?"

"Yes many times."

"Splendid. I may extend to you an invitation. Or someone may direct you here."

"Is that why you called me?"

"No, I'm calling you because America is escalating this crisis and doing more harm than good in the world. But I care for Bradley Manning, once very deeply in fact, and I listen to him when he speaks. Do you know he just returned from Miami?"

There was that city again. "No, I'm not familiar with his itinerary, but I think the world of Brad," I answered, thinking her suggestion that I might know Brad's travels peculiar at best. "Why should I know of his return from Florida?"

"Because he knows your whereabouts."

"He does?"

"Yes, he does, Brad talked about you at length, seems like they all know your status."

"Who is all?"

Dr. Faro grew frustrated; I heard it in her breaths. "By Miami, Mr. Jordan, you have no idea how powerfully informed and how far reaching they are," she said. "Their tentacles extend everywhere."

"Did Brad shed any light on Miami for you?"

"No, but I can make my own deductions."

"Then make some for me because this Miami thing is bizarre."

I was ignored once more. I heard Dr. Faro ruffle some pages. "I have your interview with Business Week in my hands and you knew this crisis was possible. You said as much, here on these pages. If the Chinese invade Taiwan, we're heading toward a nuclear holocaust because you Americans are treaty bound."

This time I ignored her. I had to go back to Miami. "Did Brad want you to call me?" I asked. "Come on, you must know something."

"Yes, I know plenty, and yes, Brad said he was instructed by Miami to have me call you. Some very important people are watching you, sir."

"Who the hell are these people?"

Dr. Faro delayed again for a few seconds. "Well, what I can tell you is that I have learned things you wouldn't believe, Mr. Jordan, fantastic things," she said. "Secrets and people of secrets and secrets never meant to be known. These are as imposing a people as the world has ever seen."

"I would love to hear—"

"Cut the repartee," she interrupted me, her tone officious and adamant. "This is no time for bullshit. You need to focus and focus now. We are in the game of the millennium, Mr. Jordan, so get off your ass while you still have an ass to get off of."

Her last comment was insulting. I had to come back at her one final time. "So far, you're just raising more questions, Dr. Faro," I snapped back, "and it's frustrating as hell. I need answers from you, not queries and hints and fantastical allusions."

"Mr. Jordan, I have some answers for you, but not as many as Miami. Open your eyes to the world around you and the opportunity given. And I'm glad you are finally showing some spunk."

"You're not going to tell me anything of value, are you?"

"I already have. But I will avoid answering you further until we meet. Know that there's unimaginable power in that town, sir, unimaginable power. Miami will prove instrumental to resolving the current crisis. And they want you involved in the biggest way."

"So you say, but I still don't have any clue what they are. So I guess I'll just wait for your invitation."

Dr. Faro whistled to herself. "You won't have to wait long," she said, "this crisis is coming to a head. When Miami gets involved, it's critical. And the next time you pencil me in for an institute, contact me directly. I had to learn of your intentions through the press. Now I must go."

And she was gone. I stood perplexed. A rare summer storm passed through the hills and rumbled eastward toward the valley village of Orinda. I watched the lightning strikes far off in the distance. Once again it seemed Miami was directing events; Nicholas, Christopher Thrattas, Bradley Manning, and now Manuela Faro were somehow connected to that southern Floridian city of newfound mystery. I thought of secrets and people of secrets and the secrets people keep. Could Miami be one big secret? And why were they always one step ahead of everybody else?

FIVE

Reuters—Lisbon, Portugal
September 6, 2017

The Portuguese ambassador to Russia, Roberto Guerra, today sought to assuage fears that biological weapons from the old Soviet arsenal had been brought to Lisbon from the arms cartel known as Carte Blanche for disposition to an unknown purchaser. Categorically denying innuendo that Lisbon was the European center for arms trafficking, Guerra reiterated that the Russian Government had accounted for all biological weaponry and that Portuguese security services had scoured the city of Lisbon and found no trace of either bio-weaponry or Carte Blanche. Still, insinuation ran rampant on a pending bio-weaponry arms deal to be completed by the middle of the month. The government of Turkmenistan today echoed the Portuguese issuing a statement claiming Carte Blanche activities in Turkmenistan had ceased to exist "for well over a year now."

The next morning, the day I was to meet Adrienne Stavenen, was a crisp-sky morning and plenty cold. Trail branches snapped at my feet as I walked alone in the woods, the winds freezing my cheeks and my hands. The storm had cleared, but a freakish cold front had followed it, rare for September. After my morning trek, I came home and noticed a yellow light flashing on the BMS system indicating activity; the heuristic software in the BMS was "clueing," occasionally scanning Eric's world and fixating on a scene if the software sensed importance. So far there had been no false alarms. I turned on the monitor and waited; the flickering of the screen was a sign the system was beginning to fail, but gradually the shapes on the monitor became more recognizable.

In front of Eric Waller sat five mostly rotund men around a large wooden table smoking cigars and drinking what appeared to be shots of vodka from an unmarked bottle. The room was very plain. As I watched, I saw that one of the men was the guy with the gray mane and devilish goatee I had seen talking with Eric in Campbell. He was seated closest to Eric and said nothing.

"I hope you enjoy the cigars," Eric said to the group, "as they come from Cuba through a personal friend of Castro."

The roundest of the men spoke from his seat at the right side of Eric. "Please give your supplier our compliments," the man said. "And the vodka is exceptional. It's the one thing the Russians do well."

The entire group shifted in their seats.

"I'm glad you approve," Eric said to the man. Glasses clinked in a toast, but no one said anything; it was more a knowing among friends.

"Shall we get down to business?" Eric asked.

"Yes, before the vodka hits," the man responded. He was a rotund, double chinned man with a shaven bald head and tiny eyes. He was older than the others, seemingly mid fifties, very dark complexioned, and the only man dressed in a business suit. His eyes scanned the room. "This crew will need another bottle," he quickly concluded.

"You're the drunk," someone threw in.

"Fuck you."

"You should hook up an IV," ribbed another.

"Did I mention fuck you?"

There were bursts of laughter.

"Not to worry," Eric stated, joining in, "there is more vodka in the back. So let's begin."

The group watched Eric make his way over to a large map on the side wall. A spotlight from the ceiling shone down on the map causing an awful glare and coupled with the cigar smoke it made for difficult viewing. It seemed to be a map of the Earth. The other men, dressed in jeans and sport coats and one with a leather jacket ripped in the shoulders, all huddled together around the bottle and helped themselves to additional shots of vodka. No one called any other man by name. Looks for order substituted for words as the smoke thickened.

"I have become quite impressed with Carte Blanche," Eric began. "There's little record of you; it's like you exist in name only."

"Anonymity has been our goal," the business suit said.

"The deposit I made in Bucharest has been verified?" Eric asked.

"It has," another man threw in.

Eric looked over the room in one sweeping glance, pulling out a laser pointer. "Good, take a look at the map," he instructed. "Remember, drop zones are points of entry. My people will take the product to their actual targets. As you can see, a red "X" identifies the drop zone."

The entire group scanned the map for probably thirty seconds and said nothing. "That seems straightforward enough," a voice at the table finally commented. I tried to make out the locations on the map, but details were blurry.

"I hope so, but our biggest concern is passing through borders unde-tected," Eric said. "Once the weapons are in-country, concealment is sim-ple. Canisters are canisters."

The man with the leather jacket spoke next. I could not see the loca-tion of the red "Xs" on the map through the smoke and glare. In fact, the blurriness was worsening. Although the BMS allowed me to see what Eric saw, the transfer to me exacerbated the haziness in the room. When the man with the leather jacket stood to speak, he blocked the map entirely.

"The American drop will prove most difficult," he began, "because security is particularly tight in the United States. The desert location is best. The drug wars have occupied border patrol for years and the authori-ties won't be looking for us."

"That's interesting," Eric commented, "what about the Middle East?"

"Tunisia is out," the man responded quickly. "So is Morocco. We can use Egypt or Sudan. We might—"

The man with the gray mane interrupted him. "Use Egypt," he said, devoid of expression. "I don't like Sudan. Too risky."

The man with the leather jacket acquiesced immediately, but the man in the business suit spoke up. "Well, if you don't want Sudan, then Cairo will cover the Mediterranean. That's no problem. But the desert location for America makes me nervous."

"Why's that?" the gray mane man asked.

"The place is swarming with border guards," the business suit answered. "They look for anything suspicious, not just drug lords."

The room went silent. Everyone peered at the map again. After a time, the gray mane man spoke. "No, we will use the desert location and you will personally make the drop. That way we know it gets done right."

The business suit smiled. "Compliment taken, so let me continue," he said, facing the group. "Macao is solid and so is Amsterdam, but I have a question regarding Rio."

Eric Waller jumped in. "I know what you're thinking. Rio increases our risk because of distance, but security in Brazil is weak and I need a drop zone for South America."

The man with the business suit spoke up again. "Our concern was you might destroy our favorite vacation city," he joked. "Use the fucker on Moscow."

The group laughed heartily again, even the gray mane man turned his head toward the others and shared in the comment. "Oh, I'm sure Mr. Waller has something planned for our Russian friends," the gray mane man said.

Eric was using his real name, his real name on Earth anyway, indicating a high level of trust. That was very worrisome.

"It may not be Moscow," Eric responded, "but the Russians will pay for their transgressions against your loved ones. You can count on that."

There was a silence of remembrance. It seemed the Russians had possibly imprisoned or killed some family members or friends of Carte Blanche. Eric sensed the recollection; I felt it in his pause. The Illick can be obsequious in their movements and speech and they learn the ways of others quickly. Eric waited an inordinately long but polite silence and said nothing to the group. The man with the leather jacket was the first to speak. His demeanor was deadly serious.

"Our hope is that the most devastating attack occurs on Russian soil. You know our past."

"I do."

I sensed palpable tension in the room. "We know an attack on America best furthers our short positions in global markets, but a hit on Russia accomplishes nearly the same thing," the leather jacket man implored. "There is after all one special canister."

Eric glanced around the room, at faces both hopeful and subordinate. "Sorry, that special canister is reserved," he said, cajoling with his words. "But don't fret; the Russians will pay dearly. Trust me."

It was at that moment I understood the extent of Eric's ruse. Eric had convinced Carte Blanche he was using biological weapons to cause a global financial meltdown while he and Carte Blanche had short positions in various stock markets around the world. It was ostensibly a money making scheme. I knew better. Eric was bent on worldwide destruction, most likely to induce various nations into blaming each other for the attacks and thereby escalating terrorism to war and then onward to global annihilation. The men in front of him were being led to a slaughter they couldn't comprehend; in the end, they would never get to spend whatever money Eric was paying them. If humanity went down in flames, these men too would be burned.

The man in the business suit spoke again. "Have you thought for example what might happen if America believes the weapons were placed by China or Russia? Might this lead to retaliatory nuclear strikes?" he asked.

"I thought of it," Eric answered, "but the probability is near zero."

"Why's that?"

"Well, because each of the biological weapons has a signature like a nuclear weapon. Experts will quickly deduce all material came from Russia and that the material was stolen years ago. These same experts will quickly point to Carte Blanche as the likely supplier. That's why you will have to reconstitute your group and shift your base of operations."

"Scrutiny will increase?"

"Hundred fold. Count on it."

"Is there any way to change signatures?"

"No, no way on Earth."

Those words were prophetic. Eric could use Illick technology to switch chemical signatures on the biological weapons. I quickly deduced this was his stratagem; by switching signatures it would appear each biological weapon had come from a different country other than Russia and that the weapons were current manufacture. Once the signatures were switched, nations would almost assuredly blame each other for the attacks and launch nuclear strikes or major ground offensives in an effort to retaliate. Moreover, a terrorist organization or arms dealer like Carte Blanche would never be suspected since it would appear each weapon had come from a sovereign state and not an international arms cartel. The world would be at war in the blink of an eye. As millions of people died from biological attack, each country would have to retaliate against the nation whose identity was the same as the signature on the weapon or face ridicule or revolution at home.

My mind raced ahead.

It wouldn't take many canisters of biological weapons to incite a conflagration. I figured seven or eight canisters would do the trick, assuming they were strategically placed in countries with sufficient retaliatory capabilities and the signature pointed to a logical adversary. The only exception was the Rio drop, unless the plan was to pit Brazil against Argentina, and that didn't make much sense. No, more likely the weapon used in South

America would be an "extinction event" weapon, presumably air borne Ebola, devastating huge populations in one sickening fait accompli.

Surprisingly, the gray mane man rose from his seat and went to the map. All eyes were on him.

"Mr. Waller, please have a seat," he stated. "My group, listen well."

Eric found a seat, as did the other men. Although the BMS transmission was hazy, I could still read body language and the gray mane man was sagging in spirits, deflating as he organized his thoughts. To his credit, he gathered himself and began.

"What you are about to hear won't be pleasant," the gray mane man said. "But we need to concern ourselves with every contingency."

At that moment, you could hear a mouse sleeping on the other side of the world. I have never heard such silence.

"Some years ago," he said, "I was approached by representatives of The Ukraine seeking material for a dirty bomb, presumably for use against Russian interests. The actual target was never determined, but the deal included high grade plastic explosives and a chemical "spreader" to increase fallout from the detonation. It was a highly effective weapon, capable of killing tens of thousands of people. At the last minute, the deal was thwarted."

"Thwarted by whom?" Eric asked, suddenly concerned.

The gray mane man shrugged his shoulders. "That was never determined, but the head of Ukrainian security and my people checked every possible organization," he said.

"What did you find?"

"Well, basically nothing. The Ukrainian cabal was comprised of what appeared to be loyal generals, but the plot was foiled from the inside. That we knew. Russian Security, CIA, Interpol, the Mossad, everyone was checked and we found no penetration by any known organization. So the best intelligence services in the world had no idea this deal was going down. Yet, we were penetrated."

"Any guesses as to who it was?" Eric asked.

"Do you remember a Belgian named Ernst Candle?" the gray mane man asked the group, before turning his head back to Eric. "Perhaps Mr. Waller, you may have heard of him as well."

Eric shook his head no, as the others in the room scanned their memories. The man with the leather jacket recalled something and nodded. "Yes, of course," he said enthusiastically, "now I remember him. He was nicknamed 'the beast,' the greatest torture master ever."

"That is correct," the gray mane man answered. "After the Ukrainian deal was compromised, the Ukrainians surmised one of their generals betrayed the cabal and Ernst Candle worked his magic on this suspected general."

"What happened?" Eric asked.

"Candle tortured him for a week in an underground facility in Kiev before the general died," the gray mane man said. "And the general uttered only one word the entire time: Miami."

The group looked puzzled. So did Eric. "What did that mean?" Eric asked.

"We think it meant the general held his allegiance to some group in Miami. Candle's methods always produced results, so 'Miami' was all this general knew. Otherwise, Candle would have gotten more out of him."

"You mean this general didn't know anything other than a contact name or city?" Eric asked

"Exactly. Even Candle was frustrated."

"You never learned more?"

"No, we never turned up anything. Somehow 'Miami' was able to stop the deal in ways we never saw coming. Their intelligence was unparalleled, uncannily accurate. And whoever they are, they may try to stop this deal as well."

The group seemed spooked. Eric sensed it. "Did you ever hear of Miami again?" he asked.

"No, I did not."

"Well then, I wouldn't worry about it," Eric said, casting a virtually hypnotic spell over the room. "It was probably a subsidiary organization created by the CIA for Ukrainian operations and Miami was the codeword. I have seen that dynamic played out before."

"You have?"

"Yes, a group masterminded for a single purpose and then quickly disbanded. In the game, they're known as a 'ghost cluster.' That's why the traitorous general only knew a codeword; that was very clever of the CIA."

The gray mane man seemed reassured, at least temporarily. "I hope you're right," he said, "since we could use a break."

Eric jumped at the chance. He smiled broadly. "Soon we will be richer than our wildest dreams. Imagine. All the money you have ever wanted. No one can stop us. Our biggest problem will be where to spend all our cash."

The group gradually nodded all around, wanting to believe.

"Fine, but let's keep our eyes and ears open," the gray mane man cautioned. "This Miami thing has had me rattled for years. I would rather not have to deal with them."

There was no chance the conversation was going to end on an admonitory note. I knew Eric and the Illick powers of persuasion all too well. He leaned in, seduction oozing from his every pore, like some femme fatale ensnaring yet another clueless sap. He made eye contact with everyone in the room. "Don't forget," he finally concluded, "the Russians suffer the medieval rack. Imagine all those boneheads gasping for air and bleeding out of every orifice of their miserable, revolting bodies."

The room was suddenly invigorated. "To us," the men toasted to Eric.

"To us," Eric toasted in return, "and to untold riches. Prepare yourselves to be the wealthiest men on Earth."

I suddenly felt sick to my stomach. Biological weapons attacks were much simpler to execute than nuclear terrorism and much more common. I had seen that in other worlds. Paradoxically, both biological and nuclear weaponry had similar fallout patterns; some years ago, I read a secret

NATO report hacked by Donald and authored ironically by Dr. Faro's technology lab in Brussels assessing cities most likely to be targeted by terrorist organizations for nuclear attacks. It was brilliant work, both materially and philosophically, and covered the most likely outcomes: initial blast devastation, wind current patterns, resulting psychological trauma, mutation frequencies, you name it, that report was as thorough as any I had ever read and I still maintained a copy in my files that I could use to pinpoint target cities. Still, that assumed Eric had examined similar reports or conducted his own studies and come to the same conclusions as the NATO findings. And he was smart enough to simply pick a random city or two just to countermand a countermeasure.

I had to stop this plot and stop it now. I needed to reread Dr. Faro's report and fully understand the factors considered in writing that report. It would help to talk to her directly. There might be a clue in such a conversation as to which cities Eric might ultimately decide to target. But first I had to talk to Donald.

* * *

The one thing I have always admired about Donald is his punctuality. He arrived exactly fifteen minutes after I phoned him. I led him from the front door into my study.

"What the hell is so damned important," he demanded, "that you couldn't just upload a report? I read them all, you know."

"Shut up and listen. How many drinks have you had?"

"One."

"One doesn't stink like that. Can you follow along with me?"

"Of course, I'm fine."

"Then go see Ambassador Wren and tell him what I've learned."

I saw a huge scowl. "That's a trip," Donald said. "What the fuck have you discovered? Nothing is that urgent."

"Yes, this is. Ambassador Wren and I set up a special signal for extreme situations some years ago."

"What signal?"

"Sending you."

"But wait, why send me?"

It was truth time, and long overdue. "Because Ambassador Wren and I suspect the Illick are close to intercepting uploads. You have too much ego involvement in your equipment to consider that possibility."

Donald sobered quickly. Knowing Ambassador Wren and I were on the same side terrified him. "Okay, so what's the problem?" he asked me skittishly.

"Eric Waller intends to launch biological weapons attacks. It will appear that humans will exterminate themselves, as the attacks will be presumed to be an outgrowth of the current crisis, with nerves already on edge."

"Are humans unwittingly involved?"

"Yes, an arms cartel is supplying Eric with the weapons."

Donald recalled something in his mind. "The Illick are masters of working with indigenous populations," he said. "We've seen that dynamic before. Humans won't suspect a thing, yet the Illick goal of eradication will be complete."

"Well said."

Donald pondered the ceiling. "Can't we enforce the treaty before the plot unfolds?" he asked, bringing his eyes to meet mine. "We have just cause."

I shook my head. "No, we gathered this information through BMS which itself is a treaty violation. We must stop them without divulgence of the implant."

Donald grinned at me. It was a grin of relief, strange for that moment. He seemed almost happy. "No, *you* have to stop the Illick," he said. "That is your job. Perhaps if you dumped that young woman from the Chronicle—"

My look interrupted Donald and told him all he needed to know. "Okay, okay, I'm leaving," he said. He rose from his seat and I followed him out to his car. He turned around and faced me after opening the driver side door. "I'll do what I can, but Ambassador Wren may want to see you himself. I think—"

"Just tell Ambassador Wren to prepare The Council for the worst."

"But I want off this dust ball. And I want my directorship."

I glared, backing him up. He got in his seat and rolled down the window. "So what should I tell the Ambassador is your plan?" he asked me.

"I meet with Stavenen today," I answered, rapping his car roof and motioning for him to leave. "Soon I will consult with Dr. Faro about her NATO report, whether she invites me to South America or not."

"We used her findings to plan CX," Donald remembered, "impressive stuff for a human. Your latest report said you might be going to Argentina."

"I might. I want her opinion on possible weapons placements."

"And what is Miami. The Council is quite concerned it may be an Illick shadow alliance."

"No, Miami has nothing to do with the Illick. It's something we haven't counted on."

Donald remembered something else. "Oh, I almost forgot to tell you," he said, proud of his recollection. "We turned a Malcurnian spy." The Malcurnians are an ally of the Illick, typically serving under Illick supervision.

"Okay, what did he say?"

"It was a she, and she informed us the Malcurnians, acting alone and this time without Illick oversight, used Wopasden Technique on some hardliner in Pakistan and another security officer as well." Wopasden Technique is advanced brainwashing, usually effective within a few hours. "The Council learned from this spy that the goal would be for this hardliner to launch nuclear weapons shortly after a coup. They figure The Council will launch CX and that's the end of human culture."

"Yes, that's the Malcurnians trying to impress their Illick masters," I quickly surmised, "but this hardliner would first have to assume power.

The Malcurnians are playing that card for the long haul. That buys us some time."

Donald crumpled his brow. He went flat as a tire. "Another complication, another mess," he complained, "I have a bad feeling about this dung heap. Earth isn't going to last, mark my words."

"Just in case, get everyone prepared," I said, stepping away from the car. "And never mention Jenny again. Now go, I have to meet with Stavenen."

SIX

Reuters—Singapore

September 6, 2017

The Singaporean government announced this evening its ambassador to Taiwan, Si Rhon Lee, has confirmed the naval blockade of Taiwan by warships of The Peoples Republic of China and that an amphibious force of over 50,000 Chinese troops, supported by massive missile strikes and naval bombardment, has landed on Taiwan's northern coast and is driving toward the capital city of Taipei. Taiwanese forces are offering bitter resistance, but were caught unexpectedly by the suddenness and ferocity of the Chinese attack and are expected to be quickly overrun. The American Pacific Fleet dispatched a naval battle group spearheaded by two aircraft carriers and an undisclosed number of nuclear submarines to Taiwan.

The University of California at Berkeley is a hilly campus. The only sounds were the gurgling of creeks and the occasional bike being racked. Mist hangs in the trees and the grounds swale like roller coasters; pretty trestle bridges made of lumber jams and train rails straddle every stream and every forecourt eventually conjoins a pillow of lawn. It's like the old world met the new. So down the hills I walked until I passed through the iron spires of ancient Sather Gate where I soon came to a stone building with the word "HISTORY" chiseled high in marble above its archway.

The hallway leading to Dr. Stavenen's office was dimly lit and smelled musty. A wholesome looking girl with curly brown hair milled about with a tall blond fellow and she noticed my confusion as to the whereabouts of Dr. Stavenen's office.

"Are you lost?" the young woman asked me.

"Trying to find Dr. Stavenen's office," I replied.

"Three doors down on the right," she said, pointing the way. "It's her office hours until noon."

"Are you a student of hers?"

"I was. Say something favorable about the United Nations and how it needs money."

"Thanks, I'll try to remember that."

"One final thing," the girl interjected. I turned around to face her again. "With the Chinese invading Taiwan, she's likely a bear today. Stavenen has her moods. Straka convened an emergency session this morning, so don't piss her off."

My look must have conveyed my anxiety and the two students gathered their things and left the building with glances that commiserated. I made my way to Dr. Stavenen's office and knocked on her door.

"Come in," I heard a woman's voice say inexpressively.

I opened the door.

Behind a large round table littered with coffee cups, a half-eaten glazed donut and a sizeable stack of manila folders sat a diminutive middle-aged woman with the surmising gray eyes of an arctic wolf. Her hair was short cut blond and messy. I quickly noticed her body seemed much too small for a person of her stature. She hurriedly folded her laptop and fastened it with a resounding click. She squinted and firmed her view, as a shooter sights a target. I saw on her nose a recent surgical scar, still puffy and a bit reddened.

"Hi, I'm David Jordan."

The woman rose and offered a handshake. I noted an almost imperceptible hollowness underneath her energy, closely akin to sadness. She never once took her eyes off me, but her gaze softened and her face relaxed.

"I'm pleased to meet you," she said agreeably, "I'm Dr. Adrienne Stavenen."

"Nicholas Straka sends his best."

"Like hell he does. He's a misogynistic bastard and I hate his guts."

"How do you really feel?" I joked.

Dr. Stavenen was not amused. "Straka is a dinosaur. He's a slob and a cheat and his mistress is an idiot. I overlooked that to bring you here. Your work is important, the geopolitical situation grave. May I call you David?"

"Sure, I'd prefer that."

"Good. Then David it is. And at the end of our time today, I have a surprise for you."

"Oh really, what surprise?"

"No, at the end of our day. Not before. And I hope you're open minded."

Before I could comment, Dr. Stavenen returned to her seat and I took the seat offered me. I sat directly across from her. She moved a stack of folders to the side, still eyeing me, while her face grew serious without loosing its comfort.

"Now listen and listen closely," she started. "Stanley M. Kerr, a life-long friend of mine and our ambassador to Singapore, informed me the American 7th Fleet is en route assisting the Taiwanese in defending their island. This is getting worse by the hour."

"I know President Rice said America will honor its treaty obligations and use all force necessary. That usually means the nuclear option."

Dr. Stavenen threw her head back, eyeing the ceiling fan. She stirred her hair.

"There's more to the story," she said, refocusing on me. "The Chinese are massing on the border with India, with over a million troops. They have tank divisions, artillery, and oodles of planes."

"Preparing for a ground invasion?"

"Count on it. And Pakistan is advancing in Kashmir. India is about to be pinched."

"Most experts predict the Kashmiri conflict advances to nuclear war if either side is quickly defeated."

"Scary isn't it?"

"Well, that's why I'm here to see you," I commented, trying for a little levity.

Dr. Stavenen sat stone faced. She fussed with her hair again. "Be realistic, David, as I'm sure you'll leave here disappointed."

"Why's that?"

The sun went behind a cloud and then came out again, the shifting light spotlighting Dr. Stavenen's next comment.

"History is the past interpreted, nothing more," she said, again rather dully. "There's no magic to it. History is full of lessons, but rarely any solutions."

"I guess we're starting the interview."

"It started when you first walked through my door. Straka and the people directing him are about to get their way. I will tell you what I know, but you must know that Straka is not really in charge of much."

I did know that. Most leaders in the world are figureheads. It's the cabals and secret elites who usually run things. I looked around. I hadn't realized until then that Dr. Stavenen's office took an entire corner of the building and was much larger than I first imagined. A clerestory window viewed outward to the creeks; in the foreground was a pretty rose garden, as lovely as a painting. I felt peace and started my conversation.

"Dr. Stavenen," I began, "what are the root causes of human conflict?" It seemed a safe question to begin with.

Dr. Stavenen's eyes regained some life; they actually twinkled and she took only the briefest of moments before she answered my query. "You're familiar with the Hegelian Dialectic?"

"Yes."

"Good, then you know ideas shape history. A thesis is challenged by its antithesis and from their struggle comes a synthesis of the two ideas.

This synthesis becomes a higher order thesis of its own, challenged by yet another antithesis, also of a higher order, and the process continues unabated. Nations essentially play out this same dynamic. This is the dialectic. Capitalism versus Communism, the world against Nazism, China versus America. Call it progress if you will."

"Is the word *unfolding* appropriate?"

Dr. Stavenen frowned. "No, the dialectic is more than an unfolding," she said. "Unfolding is inherently devoid of meaning. And I hesitate to use that term."

"What term?"

Dr. Stavenen placed her elbows on the table, her hands in the classic cupped position, seemingly beholding truth. "*Meaning*, David, we all want there to be meaning."

"You are saying history moving toward a final goal or outcome?"

"Exactly, and that is known as teleology. Although I must point out most academics deny teleological law as man's fantasy, a sort of last grasp at the straw of meaning. They also largely deny any historical laws. To them physics has proven the fundamental randomness of the universe, with no grand design."

"Do you agree there is no grand design?"

Dr. Stavenen didn't hesitate. "No, but the dialectic is irrefutably propelling man toward the current crisis, where humans are randomly at each other's throats and thus seemingly devoid of design."

"Because what design would construct its own destruction?"

"Absolutely. When Taiwan falls and India is outmaneuvered, nukes will fly. Chaos is inevitable; people are already looting and shooting each other."

"People are giving up hope?"

It was obvious Dr. Stavenen's preferred style was rapid fire, yet for the first time she hesitated. "Yes, hope is waning, and that's why you're here," she finally said. "Society is crumbling. Soon, anarchy will reign."

"It's too bad there aren't more concrete laws of history. Laws would help at a time like this." I saw Dr. Stavenen grow pleased, like a hunter firing the perfect shot. She waited for me to be struck.

"Okay," she said, almost bubbling. "Now we're at my laws."

*　*　*

Dr. Stavenen's office brightened as more fog burned off and the sun moved higher in the sky. Bells chimed off in the distance and Dr. Stavenen walked to the clerestory window and gazed outside. She quickly returned and took her seat.

"Do you see those students in the rose garden?" she asked me.

"Yes."

"Notice how they're grouped together."

Of the twenty or so students in the garden only one sat off by himself. The rest were in groups of three and four, sometimes two, and the one solitary young man soon waved to a friend passing by on the concourse.

"Man is a social animal," Dr. Stavenen began, "whether in large or small groups. Social relationships are the outcome of man's physical needs for food, shelter, and reproduction. Societies organized as a result. Sound good so far?"

"Yes."

"The survival drive is paramount to human existence, superseding all other motivations. It forces us into conflict with other societies in competition for the world's scarce resources."

"Geopolitics. That makes sense."

"Then it follows that the organizing principle behind every society is for war."

"Wait a minute, that's far too simplistic," I objected. "That's not even a novel idea."

Dr. Stavenen smugly lifted her gaze. "You asked what the march of ideas through history says about human conflict," she reiterated, "so here it is: *scarcity mandates humans will forever be in conflict for scarce resources.*"

I debated in my head whether to ask my next question. Yes won.

"What if a planet had sufficient resources for all of its inhabitants?"

Dr. Stavenen stared at me in disbelief. "You mean what if there was no scarcity?"

"Yes."

Dr. Stavenen rubbed her temples and then her eyes. She seemed caught off guard. "Well, astronomers here at Cal have found extra-solar planets revolving around distant stars, but I can't imagine a planet where there is completely sufficient resources."

"Such planets exist, trust me."

The smugness was gone, replaced by genuine curiosity. "Okay, but it doesn't seem likely a planet would be sufficiently stocked with enough natural resources to last forever," she commented.

I wasn't through. "What if an intelligent species on such a planet controlled its population to match the planet's resources or developed technologies making its resources nearly inexhaustible?"

Dr. Stavenen raised an eyebrow. "I guess that's possible, but you'd still be left with the original survival drive. Although perhaps—well, I suppose the survival drive could be bred out or curtailed in the event of unlimited resources, but now we're into science fiction. That is of course unless you know something I don't know."

Dr. Stavenen came forward in her chair once more and peered into my eyes. At that precise moment, a ray of sunlight came pouring in through the window and shined directly into my face. Dr. Stavenen scrutinized my eyes and her mouth went agape.

"Do you know when the sun shines into your eyes you have—"

"Yes, a genetic anomaly," I said hastily, "it's been described as a golden flecking. It's been there my whole life. I'm sorry for hypothesizing as I did, now please continue."

Dr. Stavenen rose from her chair and walked around it, eyeing me the entire time. The sun went behind a cloud and the room darkened again. Satisfied, she returned to her seat. "Well then," she resumed, still scanning me, "my next law of history is a simple one: *history is a recordation of the survival drive.* The survival drive plays itself out as an economic struggle for the world's scarce resources."

"Economic Darwinism."

I saw a slight nod. "And here's how," she said. "Men by nature possess different capabilities and talents and the resulting complexity of social life caused uneven distribution of goods and services. Without enough to go around, hierarchies and exploitation resulted. GATDP and the Chinese reaction is a continuation of historical competition to control the world's scarce resources."

My look conveyed my willingness to listen to more without questioning. The woman in front of me seemed pleased; she took another gulp of coffee and smiled at me. "My next law is also simple," Dr. Stavenen continued. "*History is moreover social systems recognizing the primacy of the survival drive.*"

I found this comment to be a curious one. "Governments have not admitted that fact," I remarked, "none that I know of anyway."

Dr. Stavenen simpered. "True, what government wants to admit the survival drive is predominant and thus there will always be ceaseless competition for the world's scarce resources? In other words, there will never be enough to go around?"

"No government would admit that, it might encourage revolution."

"Which is why virtually every society has tried to redistribute wealth."

Her points and linkages were brilliant. What she didn't know was that the same dynamic occurs in many civilizations throughout the galaxy; some survive, some do not. Humans were on the precipice.

"So governments do enough to keep their societies placated and then they compete against other societies for the world's scarce resources," I said. "And the root is—"

"Our unrestrained survival drive. That should be clear by now. It is the source of human conflict. China, India, America, all simply following their base natures, their DNA extrapolated up to the geopolitical level, trying to survive in a highly competitive environment. And this time, it may cause a nuclear war."

I changed discs on my recorder and waited for her to continue while I absorbed her message.

Humans seemed further than ever from saving themselves.

All I saw was innocence lost.

* * *

"We are now at my final law of history," Dr. Stavenen said, rather abruptly. "And this law is inviolable: *history reflects the cyclical nature of the universe, the dynamic of rise and fall, and it applies for nations, for civilizations, and indeed for people themselves.*"

"So humans are doomed?"

"We are almost assuredly finished as a species."

I couldn't imagine a bolder statement coming from such a public figure. For some reason, it angered me. "Dr. Stavenen, that's preposterous," I snarled at her, "it goes against all public relations decorum. In fact, it is outlandish. I'll just turn my recorder off."

Dr. Stavenen rose from her chair and shot me a dagger. "Don't you dare erase a single word," she reprimanded, before sitting back down. "I know us public figures are supposed to keep up appearances, but I want Mr. Straka and the rest—"

"But Dr. Stavenen, you need data to back up such a conclusion. You'll be ridiculed by everyone in academia, not to mention assailed by the public for a lack of compassion. I can't report that opinion back to Nicholas Straka. He, along with everyone else, will want some kind of proof."

"Oh, I have proof, David. I have developed with Dr. Walton Cooley here at Cal a heuristic computer model 99.865% accurate and in academia any number greater than 95% is considered proof. The world will see for itself next month."

"Boy, I can't wait for that news conference."

"Sure, laugh now," she scolded, her arms crossing in front of her chest. "But the world is living on borrowed time. The end of utopian models, both communism and capitalism, has already occurred. The survival drive is subsuming international relations like a giant python swallowing a rat."

"Civilizations have clashed for millennia."

"Never with so many of them armed with nuclear weapons. And give me one historical example where a weapon invented is not also a weapon eventually used en masse?"

That was an excellent point, well-taken and scary. Weapon systems are used to their full destructive potential until replaced by something superior. It's a galactic axiom.

"What about globalization?" I finally asked, playing devil's advocate. "Some say it's bringing the world together."

Dr. Stavenen eyed me with a mixture of ridicule and regret. "Okay, let me get this straight: more advanced economies with more advanced militaries all competing for ever scarcer resources? Tell me that's not a recipe for war."

I glanced at my notes. I was looking for holes in her logic. "Okay, you mentioned the model is 99.865% accurate," I said. "If my math is correct, that means humanity has a .135% chance of surviving."

"Correct."

"Did the model say anything about time?"

"Not really. The model said the probability of nuclear war is nearly 100% and 90% likely within the next decade."

I put down my pen and pad and leaned forward, full of contempt. "I'm curious about one thing," I asked. "If the model is so pessimistic, why do you believe so strongly in the United Nations?"

Dr. Stavenen's eyes burned a dancing fire. Blue eyes don't often dance, more apt to soothe or cajole, but her eyes danced and the fire was unmistakable.

"Because I want to believe in that .135% chance," she said. "And the United Nations is still the best hope. This time, those bastards are going to have to listen to me."

I remembered reading that Dr. Stavenen had a number of policy proposals rejected by the U.N., some dismissed as recently as the last few weeks. It had been front page news in many newspapers.

"So your ego was bruised?" I asked.

"Now I see why you and Straka are friends."

We said nothing to each other. I'm sure we both felt insulted. The peace of the rose garden had been shattered like broken glass. I wanted to leave, but I thought of Nicholas, my duty, and The Council. When that didn't work, I thought of Jenny.

"Forgive me," I finally managed. "I'm sorry if I hurt your feelings. But your forecast just seems so damn bleak."

Dr. Stavenen rubbed the scar on her nose. It seemed to ease her. "Forgiven," she eventually said, exhaling, "hell, I'm as frustrated as you are. I cannot believe we have all spiraled down into this soup."

The interview was nearly concluded. But Dr. Stavenen had a surreptitious strategy of sorts, something more she wanted to say, or perhaps something she wanted to pry out of me. I sensed her struggling.

"Can you turn off your tape recorder? We're done with the official interview."

"Sure."

Dr. Stavenen glanced at her watch before rifling through a stack of papers. She found the one she wanted and then ambled over to a small metal file cabinet. There, she pulled a manila folder from a drawer and after some searching yanked another piece of paper from it and placed that paper together with the first sheet drawn from the stack on the table. She came back to her chair and sat down, her hands trembling. Her lower lip quivered as she spoke.

"We have been a bit contentious today," she said. "But I'm not an insensitive bitch, you know; I apologize if I was short with you."

I waited and felt a draft of fresh air from the partially opened lower window. It felt good to breathe in some freshness.

"I can tell you have more to say," I said reassuringly, "so please go on."

Dr. Stavenen took the top piece of paper and laid it out on the table, written side up, and rotated it so that it faced me, easy to read. It was some kind of medical report and I saw the word cancer and various treatment recommendations and then signatures at the bottom of the page. I looked up and Dr. Stavenen spoke before I could ask any questions.

She pointed to the surgical scar on her nose. "This little blotch here was the most obvious of my malignancies," she said disconsolately. "The doctors don't know how long I have to live. I'd rather you keep this disclosure between us until I depart this Earth."

I fell back in my chair, stunned. "Of course," I said, searching for more to say. "This must be a difficult time. Is there anything I can do?"

Dr. Stavenen showed me the other piece of paper, never letting go of the page. "Don't read this," she insisted, "it's a letter from my son. He's in naval intelligence, my only child, graduated first in his class from Annapolis. I want there to be a world for him."

Dr. Stavenen yanked the paper back. All I saw was the naval insignia at the top. I think that was all Dr. Stavenen wanted me to see of the letter. It was her way of offering proof she had a son in the navy.

"I'll do my best," I promised. "And thank you again for your time."

Dr. Stavenen motioned for me to remain seated. It was obvious I had missed the point. "Are you sure your recorder is turned off?" she asked me.

"Yes."

Dr. Stavenen caressed the letter in her hands. "I mentioned my son is in naval intelligence," she reiterated, "and one of the navy's finest officers. I know what you're thinking—but it's far more than maternal pride. He was selected among hundreds of candidates for a secret research project in Puerto Rico."

"Congratulations. He must be some kid."

"Naturally, he couldn't tell me much about his work," Dr. Stavenen continued, ignoring my gaucherie, "but I reminded him I'm very sick and don't have long to live."

"What did he say?"

"Well, we took an evening stroll up campus and he stopped and placed his arms on my shoulders, holding me firmly in place. It was a dark night and quite still and he lifted his eyes to the stars and said 'them.' I took it to mean beings, not stars or planets."

"Fascinating."

Dr. Stavenen looked straight at me, eyeing me rather suspiciously. "My son told me only one other thing," she said. "And then he demanded no further questioning."

"This is getting good."

Dr. Stavenen looked at me decorously. "I'll paraphrase what he said: we suspect they're watching us, some are human in appearance, only much more advanced than us, there have been crashes and recovered bodies, of course some autopsies, and their brains and eyes are fascinating," she said. "He said our national security leadership is convinced they mean no harm."

"I won't tell a soul."

Dr. Stavenen came forward again in her chair. She gulped hard. What followed may have been the toughest thing she ever had to say.

"David, earlier I saw golden flecking in your eyes," she said imploringly. "Are you what I think you are?"

Directives are part of life; some are internal and some are placed on us. I always struggle with mine. I rose from my chair and made my way around the far edge of the table and came over and stood next to Dr. Stavenen.

"You didn't see anything that can't be explained."

Her entire body quavered. Dr. Stavenen put her hand to her mouth. "But are you, my God, are you from the stars?" she asked me.

"Give me your hand, I promise I am no danger to you."

Dr. Stavenen gave me her hand. She gazed up at me in a wobbly expression of apprehension and trust.

"I have a job to do," I said straightforwardly, "and so do you. If you think your computer model will inspire remedial action, I pray you're correct. Humans need to solve their own problems here on Earth. Mankind must avoid knowing what he shouldn't know before the appropriate time. Does that make sense to you?"

Dr. Stavenen was so disheveled I worried for her. "No," she stammered, "well maybe it does, I don't know."

I waited for her to gather herself. "All I know is I don't want to die and leave my son," she said, tearing up.

I violated a directive. "Do you know the power of The One?"

Dr. Stavenen wiped her tears away. She seemed confused. Her eyes were reddened and vulnerable and she wilted in her chair.

"No, I don't know, do you mean God, what does that—"

"Close your eyes." I held her hand more firmly in mine and beseeched the ageless power of The One. Dr. Stavenen closed her eyes. Her body vibrated from the energy of the moment. Her eyes opened slowly and she looked at me in amazement.

"I'm confident your health will improve," I told her. "You will probably live much longer than your prognosis. Enjoy time with your son, but never ask him again of his work. Now I must leave."

I let go of Dr. Stavenen's hand and picked up my tape recorder and notepad from the table and made my way toward the office front door.

"One more thing, David," Dr. Stavenen said sweetly, pleading with me. I looked back at her. Just a few minutes before, she had been terse and argumentative. Now she was kind and motherly. She made some clicks with her computer mouse and then looked up at me.

"I have just sent Dr. Robert Allen Gibson an email requesting his time for your next interview," Dr. Stavenen said. "I was instructed to do this if our time went well. Remember the surprise I promised you?"

I was astonished. "Instructed by whom?" I asked, disregarding the mention of her earlier promise.

"By Miami," she said, "that's what I call them. They wanted us to meet."

"You received an email?"

"Yes, a number of them. They informed me they had directed Straka to have you come talk to me. Then yesterday they also sent a letter and a digitized voice message apprising me of one David Jordan and your mission for the United Nations. They seem to know everything about both you and Straka."

"Miami again," I said, ruminating.

"You know them?"

I paused at her door. Dr. Stavenen stared at me, perplexed. "Yes, I know them," I finally said, "and my hope is that Miami is that .135% chance. I just don't know what it is they want."

I thought I would leave, but Dr. Stavenen's eyes once again flashed for me to remain. I spun a half circle to face her more directly, noticing that she seemed strangely energized, almost jubilant. "You know, I read you're a bachelor," she said, leaning back in her chair. "You should try love sometime. There's better than a .135% chance it will make you happy."

I paused, genuinely astounded at the woman seated in front of me. "Whatever made you say that?" I asked her.

Dr. Stavenen smiled the broadest smile of the day. "I'm not sure," she said, "it just came to my thoughts. The universe does that sometimes. Love is a great teacher, David."

For some reason, I didn't respond. I simply waved a friendly goodbye and made my way out the door and onto the campus again. I traipsed the hilly grounds and eventually made my way back toward College Avenue to where I had parked my car, wondering of Miami and what these humans called love.

SEVEN

Associated Press—Rome, Italy
September 6, 2017

The Italian government today released a photograph and a short biography of the man Italian security services believe is the head of the international arms cartel known as Carte Blanche. The man, Joseph Turner Abrille, is a Lebanese native and an alleged resident of Turkmenistan since 2001. His mother, Patricia Colleen Turner, is a former British radical who married former Hezbollah resistance fighter Ahmed Abrille in 1968. Ahmed Abrille was killed by Israeli military forces in a 1996 raid and Patricia Colleen Turner was found murdered in Beirut two years later. The government of Turkmenistan denies Joseph Turner Abrille is a current resident or moves freely with a government issued travel waiver. Likewise, the government of Lebanon reports Abrille has not been seen in their country since the mid 1990s and they have issued warrants for his arrest.

At home contemplating a possible trip to England, I read the press release on Joseph Turner Abrille from the Italian government and quickly contacted my friend Lance Weston, a Middle East analyst and expert at MI6 and a personal friend who might know something of Abrille.

"Hello Lance, this is David. How are you?"

"David, what the hell, it's two in the morning," he said, obviously groggy and disturbed by the hour. "This better be urgent."

"It is, and I hate to bother you. Say, I may be in London soon."

"Well call me when you get here."

"No, I need you now," I said chuckling. "I know it's late, but I want the most current information you have."

I heard Lance stagger around. "My wife is visiting family in Devonshire or she'd have your guts for garters," he said, still bleary. "So what's so damn important that couldn't wait until tomorrow?"

"What do you know about Joseph Turner Abrille?"

"Damn, this is serious. Hang on."

I did as directed. In a couple of minutes my email alert toned.

"Did you receive my email attachment," Lance asked, back on the call.

I checked. There was a composite drawing of Abrille bearing a striking resemblance to the gray mane man I saw with Eric Waller in Campbell. The image also matched closely the photograph released by the Italian government. It had to be him.

"Got it," I said. "What can you tell me about this guy?"

"This chap is one bad egg," Lance said, clearing his throat. "Like the Italians, we believe he's the head of Carte Blanche. They stole biological weapons from the old Soviet arsenal and our latest intelligence confirms they have a dirty bomb as well."

"That's bad news."

"Oh, there's more to the story. Russian Security penetrated Carte Blanche and nearly killed Abrille, but instead their agent was discovered and then found savagely beaten a few days later."

"Where did this happen?"

"Baku, on the Caspian Sea."

"Anything else?"

"Only that the agent died of his wounds, but not before he revealed to his Russian handlers that Abrille had a cadre of highly dedicated former Turkmenistan army officers in his inner circle who serve as his personal security and terrorist cohorts. As revenge for the death of their agent, the

Russians killed the wives and mistresses of Abrille's inner circle. Videos were made and left purposely behind."

"You're kidding me?"

"No, the murders were particularly gruesome; all the women were sodomized, mutilated, or beheaded. MI6 was appalled at the barbarity."

"It's a wonderful world."

"Isn't it? David, be careful, this Abrille is a madman. He and his cadre despise the Russians, but their hatred of Americans isn't far behind."

"What else can you tell me?"

I heard some drawers slam. "Hang on, I'm pulling his file from my desk here," Lance said. "Yes, here it is, let's see now, for the past few months Abrille has met with someone named Eric Waller. Heard of him?"

I had to lie. "No, what can you tell me about this Eric Waller?" I responded.

"Well, not much. We only suspect that's his name through a tapped phone conversation Abrille had with his top lieutenant, a killer named Karakzov. We also have two photos of a man we believe might be Waller: in the first photo he's with Abrille and in the second he's with a Russian arms dealer named Sharpova."

"Where were these photos taken?"

"Well, here's where it gets bizarre. The first photo is taken in Marseilles and the second in St. Petersburg, only two hours apart. Plane flights between those two cities take four hours minimum, not counting check in and baggage claim. Our man was on him in Marseilles, but lost his trail."

Eric must have made the two separate meetings by using an Illick planetary craft; that was risky, but much faster than human airplanes. I had to play dumb. "What, that's impossible," I threw at Lance. "You must have your times wrong."

"No, we don't think so. We know exactly when the photos were taken. But more interesting is that we checked all flight records for Eric

Waller, every airline in the world for the past six months, and there are no records of him."

I stalled for a minute, feigning pensiveness. The Illick could hack into the airlines database and erase Eric's passenger record anytime they chose. I was sure they had done just that. "Must be someone else in the second photo who looks like him," I added.

"Must be." Lance sounded like he was trying to convince us both. "Our computer analyzed the two photos and we figured about 85%-90% match up on the Waller images, but that still leaves a fairly large margin of error."

I had to seem interested. "Send me the two photos," I requested, "so at least I'll have them in my files. You never know; maybe I'll run into Waller myself."

"Will do, but do me a favor and keep this confidential. I know you're cleared for communication with MI6, but I'd still rather keep this quiet."

"I appreciate it Lance. I have to run; some equipment is acting up."

I hung up promptly. Lance Weston is as good a man as they make. I owed him one.

*   *   *

On the BMS before me, Eric Waller once again stood in front of a small group of men I didn't recognize. They were seated in chairs around a conference room table, in a high tech looking office without computers or other technological apparatus, the office incredibly drab, seemingly purposefully so. There weren't even any pictures on the walls.

I scrutinized the images.

Something seemed amiss.

None of these men were the ones I saw before discussing the weapons drops. Abrille and his cronies were missing. I watched their movements very closely: the minor hesitation when moving the head; the tongue filling in through clenched teeth; and the pinky rub of the nose when the index finger was closer and more natural to use.

Any of these attributes would usually pass unnoticed, but as a group each characteristic was accentuated in the same way a school of Basslet more clearly demonstrates reef behavior than any single fish could manage on its own. If one knew what to examine, it was impossible to misdiagnose.

These were Illick.

The drabness of the office was designed to mimic their facilities on Illician, their home planet, known throughout the galaxy for their sterility and absence of color. I should have recognized that fact immediately. Yet the table was of human design, so these Illick were still on Earth.

At that moment Eric Waller began to speak.

"Has anyone been compromised?"

"So far, we're invisible" said one of the Illick, almost dismissively. He was dressed in jeans and a pullover sweater and although I didn't recognize him, he seemed familiar. He had an ego.

"Well, let's not get cocky," Eric said. "It's not only humans we must consider, but also David Jordan. I feel his presence. It's as if he's watching us."

"Impossible," another Illick shouted. "The Council is woefully inept. David Jordan was lucky in the past."

Eric shot him a look. "Lucky?" he asked derisively. "He tracked me down in Campbell when I doubled my usual security measures. He's good, their best. Never underestimate him."

"Well, I'm more worried about Carte Blanche and their loose lips," another Illick said. "I don't trust Abrille."

Eric flexed his neck. He looked the group over. "Why, he seems plenty hoodwinked to me?" he asked.

"Because he's human," the Illick retorted, "and humans talk too much. Something tells me he's told people outside of his circle about our deal. He also accepted your ruse much too eagerly; that makes me nervous."

"You are concerned he turned down better offers to sell the weapons to us?"

"Yes."

"I see your point, that is concerning."

Another pause followed. Eric turned in the direction of another Illick and the group held its breath.

"What's your opinion Anthony?"

Anthony, the Illick in jeans and a pullover sweater, ground his teeth before he spoke.

"I think it is *Linust*."

Linust is an Illick word for a non issue, connoting a lack of concern or ambivalence. I was surprised he used it. It was a clue to his race and violated standard operating procedure. Even in a room full of Illick, it was indicative of extreme arrogance and Eric was sure to notice.

"We must remember we are superior planners," Anthony went on, "and The Council are a collection of idiots. We outsmarted them on Bacced and Wakhfrae 4 and now it's Earth's turn to suffer."

That haughtiness was unmistakable. Anthony was Anthony Rembacule, an engineer specializing in weapons systems and counter-intelligence. He graduated exemplar from the Illick Military Institute in Austenza and later founded the business and government amalgam known as a *Gesgenisthu*, serving on the most important boards. Brilliant and methodical, he had free pass throughout the galaxy and was extremely dif-ficult to track; The Council lost surveillance of him over a year ago. But we had our suspicions Rembacule was instrumental in the uprisings of Bacced and Wakhfrae 4; both of those civilizations were currently Illick allies and would probably remain so. Now we had our proof.

"Your RP procedure worked well," Eric said to Rembacule. "But I'm in charge here and I won't tolerate overconfidence."

RP was cellular transfiguration changing physical appearance on purpose; that's why I hadn't recognized Rembacule at first.

Eric walked over to Anthony Rembacule and made a temple with his fingers. It was the classic Illick gesture of solidarity and commitment to cause. The other Illick came over to Eric and took turns doing the same. When finished, they all stood and nodded to one another.

"Eric is right," Anthony said to the group, "and I apologize for my cockiness. The humans must die. That is goal number one. Their rate of development is the only one to exceed our own. Once they annihilate themselves, we will be the envy of the galaxy."

The group nodded again in unison.

The point Rembacule alluded to regarding the rate of development is known as Star Rule 1. Virtually all civilizations are at different levels of advancement because regions of the galaxy were formed in different eras of time. Older civilizations are more powerful as they are further along their evolutionary continuums and thus militarily superior, but in an effort to "catch up" younger civilizations are obsessed with the rate of progress. The faster the rate, the quicker the gap can be closed.

My BMS system flickered again and the system strained and groaned. It didn't have much life left in it. I had to rap it hard once and I thought I might lose the connection, but then Eric reappeared.

"Human progress will be circumvented by biological warfare," Eric said, the group returning to their seats. "Their unique brain chemistry will not save them this time."

Earth's special magnetism accelerates human brain development and is quite rare in the galaxy; the special magnetic effect also increases polarity and causes human duality. At some point in the future, the negative could surpass the positive and result in unrestrained warfare leading to nuclear annihilation. GADTP and the Chinese reaction might prove such a time.

"Yes, their darkness is becoming dominant," Rembacule added, directly on cue. "We have waited for this moment in history and it is upon us."

The group again nodded all around. I sensed a growing confidence, especially noticeable since the moment Eric asserted himself against Rembacule; the Illick love hierarchy and clear delineation of personal superiority excites them. But Anthony had been correct about human darkness; humans war against themselves, rare in the galaxy, especially for an advanced species. Such species rarely survive. That excited the Illick even more.

Eric positioned himself at the head of the table. "This is our last meeting before the weapons are delivered and I want no delays," he said. "Has everyone taken their serum antidotes?"

"We have," an Illick said, "with no apparent side effects."

"Good, then the final concern is activation. Chris, it's your show now."

Chris rose from his seat, scooting the chair backward with the back of his legs. I didn't recognize him.

"Abrille made the preparations to my satisfaction," Chris began. "The weapons are in route and Abrille agreed to forgo his final payment until later."

"Are you sure the weapons are being delivered?" Eric asked.

"I'm sure. We tagged them. The beacons are transmitting as we speak."

Eric thought of something. "How long do the beacons last?" he asked. "I don't want electronic emissions from their placements. They could be tracked."

Rembacule jumped in. "When the weapons are positioned at their target locations, the beacons are disabled. I saw to that."

"Good, that's proactive thinking," Eric said, "now what about security in the drop zones?"

"We flew all the drop zones last night," Chris responded, "spectrally panned with heat sensors and the latest carbon detection; none of the zones have added extra security personnel."

"We're any of our craft seen?" Eric asked.

"Only in one instance, where NATO headquarters scrambled two fighter jets to intercept us near Amsterdam, but they found nothing and returned to base. We're clear."

"Then we're ready," Eric said confidently. "All of you, job well done."

"Destruction," someone yelled.

"Death to the monkeys," screamed another.

Eric waved his hands to calm the group. "If our mission is successful," he said, "we can kiss this water rock goodbye."

"A home for pond algae," Rembacule added gleefully.

Everyone formed a temple with their fingers.

My God, how I hate the Illick.

* * *

I checked my computer before retiring to bed for correspondence that may have come while using my BMS and sure enough I had received an e-mail from Robert Allen Gibson confirming a meeting in England within the following few days.

The e-mail told me much about the man:

Dear Mr. Jordan:

This e-mail confirms my response to Dr. Stavenen's request for a discussion. Notwithstanding my reservations regarding the practicality of your agenda, I will be honored to serve the United Nations in whatever capacity I may. Next Monday is best and I have taken the liberty to schedule a sumptuous working breakfast for us, Americanized of course, with pancakes and imported maple syrup from the insurrect colony of Vermont. We'll have so precious few hours to blether. My secretary will forward security and meeting details to you within the hour. Under no circumstances are you to be encumbered by recording devices or camera, although you will be permitted to take notes. Hoping you possess a fine memory.

In failing health,

Robert Allen Gibson

I sure hoped London had good weather. The last time I flew into Heathrow we nearly crashed. Or at least it felt that way. And linear travel the human way takes next to an eternity. Not to mention boring. Still, I made my flight and hotel reservations online and sent Jenny a goodnight text and received an immediate response from her. Somehow, she had arranged for her business trip to China to include a stopover in London the day after I interviewed Dr. Gibson and she was persistent in wanting to see me. We were to spend the day together before she flew on to Beijing for her work assignment interviewing Mien Jinkao, the Chinese democratic reformer. So I uploaded a report to Ambassador Wren and packed my things for England. My last thought of the night was the worsening global crisis and of unnecessary trips made to China in a world gone increasingly violent and mad; strangely, I dreamed of my hills and clawing at the roots of trees as well as feelings of untold emptiness and despair. In the morning I felt uneasy and worried. But, as always, duty called, so I made haste to the British Isles in search of physics and global peace, and when the flight attendant mentioned our bumpy weather was clearly better than the small hurricane hitting Miami, I just laughed to myself.

EIGHT

Associated Press—New York, United States
September 8, 2017
The People's Republic of China today announced the occupation of Taiwan after a broadly successful military campaign that overran Taiwanese government forces during the past two days. Western analysts are stunned at the rapidity at which Chinese forces decimated the island's defenders. The U.S. 7th Fleet is due to arrive in Taiwanese waters within the next few hours.

A diplomatic source in Tel Aviv confirmed an Israeli air strike against an Iranian nuclear facility in Busheher today after a similar attack on another nuclear facility at Natanz in northern Iran yesterday. The U.N. Security Council, already in emergency session, vowed to discuss both the Israeli-Iranian situation and the Chinese occupation of Taiwan in today's meeting.

Oxford is the old world: quaint, cobbled, proper, and with a discernable snobbery in the air. I sensed it when I walked. Rarely did I see a smile. The mood is not necessarily somber, but rather more an exercise in the rigors. The university itself is monumental; it rises and sprawls and commands all at once, and it seemed as I walked under stately Scots Pine that all knowledge everywhere once began at Oxford. And its resident grandeur was waiting to see me inside of an hour.

So I made sure I was prompt.

The Royal Astronomical and Physics Institute sits adjacent to campus up a series of stone risers broken only by the occasional tiled courtyard separating the stairs from the patios. Low vines and ivy clung to most everything. My steps clicked as I ascended. At the top, the institute was nearly hidden by a large circle of chestnut trees and I was still noticing their intricate leaves when I heard a voice come up suddenly from behind me.

"You must be David Jordan, the American," the voice said.

I turned around, expecting to see Dr. Gibson. Instead, I saw three young men, all in military uniforms, the one speaking a captain in the Royal Navy and the other two split behind him in formation. I perceived tension apart from typical military demeanor.

"That's correct," I said amiably, "I'm David Jordan."

"Do you have some identification?" the captain asked me.

"Sure." I pulled out my passport and card.

The officer took my paperwork, looked it over, and handed it back to me. "Please follow us, sir."

The captain led me through a door at the back of the institute, the two other military personnel shadowing me. When the door closed behind us we found ourselves in a large anteroom before a dimly lit hallway of offices, where the captain turned abruptly and faced me.

"I apologize for the security precaution, Mr. Jordan, but this morning MI5 received a terrorist threat targeting Dr. Gibson. On Her Majesty's orders, all targets receive special protection until further notice. Are you carrying any weapons?"

"Of course not."

The captain pulled from his pocket a device that scans for metal as well as for plastic explosives. I have been scanned many times and recognized the devices immediately. He waved his device over me, had me remove my wallet and car keys, and then handed them back to me after another brief review.

"Dr. Gibson will see you now," the captain said.

I was led down the corridor to an interior office about mid hallway. The captain knocked on the door and opened it slowly, leading me inside. There, another junior officer stood guard. The captain waved the guard out of the office and then waited patiently for a seated elderly man to finish his telephone conversation, whose wide back and crooked neck were facing us and unmistakable in their silhouette. After a few more seconds, the seated man finished his call and swiveled his chair forward to face us.

"Dr. Gibson, this is David Jordan to see you," the captain said.

"Yes, I convened him," the elderly man said, rolling his eyes while looking at me. "Assume your post outside our door."

"Yes sir," the captain said, making his way out of the room. He closed the door softly behind him.

I felt an easing of tension. "So you're David Jordan," Dr. Gibson said smiling. "You're quite a specimen, rather handsome for an American."

I noticed his trademark white buzz haircut and white stubble beard. I also noticed the room smelled gloriously of fresh pancakes and maple syrup.

"I wish the Crown had won," I joked, "damn tea party in Boston."

Dr. Gibson struggled from his seat and rose with the help of a wooden cane, extending his arthritic arm for a handshake.

"Have at some breakfast," he said amiably.

"Sounds like a plan."

Dr. Gibson motioned me to a far table in the room. He removed a white tablecloth covering generous trays of pancakes, scrambled eggs, potatoes, and piles of shredded pork. I grabbed a plate and dug into the pancakes, starving.

We took our seats and ate for a time. "Good?" Dr. Gibson finally asked me.

"Delicious," I said between gulps.

Dr. Gibson grew serious. "Taiwan has fallen to the mainland Chinese and now India has invaded Pakistan through Kashmir," he said.

"The BBC is reporting atrocities on both sides."

Dr. Gibson made a guttural sound of disgust. "The slaughter will worsen," he said, "as it does in every war. There is always another budding Gestapo somewhere."

"The Taiwanese government in exile relocated to Guam? I thought I heard that on my way over to see you."

"Yes, this morning. You Americans can protect them there. And President Khan of Pakistan was overthrown by General Haidez Ghoshanad. I met him once."

"He's a young hardliner."

"About forty, I think, sympathetic to radical Islam."

That was ominous. I remember Ghoshanad once vowed to use nuclear weapons if any land was lost to India. Now he was in power. And he might be the hardliner in Pakistan mentioned by the Malcurnian female spy Donald told me The Council had recently turned. "Ghoshanad is not afraid to use nukes," I added.

"He'll first seek the blessing of the Chinese, but the Chinese want a land battle between Pakistan and India so India doesn't directly attack China. It's a good strategy."

"Some world we have here."

Dr. Gibson groaned. "Oh, there's more my good man, loads more," he said, recoiling. "China is aiding Iran against further Israeli strikes, upping the stakes."

"Was there an announcement?"

"Sure, the usual gibberish, but it's largely irrelevant as the Chinese have already given Iran the bomb."

If true, that was another terrible development. "If the Israelis believe China has given Iran a nuclear weapon, they may attack China as well," I said. "Israel won't take any crap; they never do."

Dr. Gibson rubbed his nose. "She'll have to take some," he retorted. "Israel can't launch a ground offensive, but she can attack with nuclear weapons. It's a chain reaction and you're jolly well smack in the middle of it."

"Thanks. So are you."

Dr. Gibson chortled and then changed the subject. "You were as early as October snow," he said, his face brightening. "Punctuality is a key with me. You seem like a good bloke, so dig in for seconds and we'll get to the matter at hand."

*　*　*

Somehow, I forced more breakfast into my stomach. It wasn't easy. I don't know if Dr. Gibson saw my growing discomfort or how I slowed to an occasional nibbling, but he was ready and full of fire.

"I'm a contemporary of Feynman, Gell-Mann, Oppenheimer and Teller," Dr. Gibson began with pride. "They admired my 'Unison Theory' and called it one of the most brilliant postulations ever formulated; its applicative failures are core to Mr. Straka's current problems. We'll get to that soon enough."

"I have read your theory completely," I noted.

Dr. Gibson gave me thumbs up. "Good, then you know I predicted the world's current geopolitical travails long before anyone else," he said. "Well, all except for Manuela Faro."

"I may be seeing her soon."

"Here in England?"

"No, Dr. Faro said she might invite me to her river retreat outside Buenos Aires. I'm still waiting for her confirmation call."

Dr. Gibson sat back as if he'd been shot. I watched him rub his eyes and then shake his head from side to side. "Bloody hell, your mission is bigger than I thought," he said, turning two shades whiter than a sprinkling of salt. "What the hell kind of a bloke are you?"

"I'm not sure I follow."

"Good grief man, no one goes to the river retreat. Not Reagan or Gorbachev or Mandela or the damn Pope. Not even her favorite the Dalai Lama. It's sacred ground, that river retreat. Why the hell would she see a chap like you?"

"Urgency, I suppose. And thanks for the vote of confidence."

Dr. Gibson turned pensive, ignoring my sarcasm. He seemed as troubled as a deserter before a firing squad. "And she probably mentioned something about Bradley Manning and his returning from Miami?" he asked me.

"How the hell do you know that?"

Dr. Gibson grunted. "Because Miami is leading her as well," he said, leaning back in his chair again. "Bradley Manning encouraged me to see you only minutes after Stavenen contacted me; if convinced you're bright and forthcoming, I refer you along to Dr. Faro. But I never dreamed it would be at her river retreat on the Iguaza."

"Are you serious? You know Bradley Manning? Did he phone you?"

"Yes and yes and yes," Dr. Gibson responded. "Brad and I have consulted on numerous NATO projects together. He distrusts the Chinese as much as I do. Never repeat that. And Brad is very close to Manuela Faro; some say, he was the love of her life."

"Miami is orchestrating this whole thing?" I asked, amazed at their connectivity.

"It seems that way. God only knows who they are and what they control."

"You think Bradley Manning is Miami?"

Dr. Gibson massaged his cheeks. "Well, maybe peripherally," he said, wondering aloud. "But Miami is more than one bloody man, it's a cabal. I've run across them before."

"When was that?"

"Well, twice: the Cuban Missile Crisis in 1962 and the Reagan/ Gorbachev spat in 1985; both nearly went nuclear. Miami only intervenes in the gravest of crises."

Now I sat back in my chair. "Sounds scary as hell," I said.

"It speaks volumes about the mess we're in."

We both paused and thought. I heard a guard shuffle outside the door. "Miami," I finally whispered to Dr. Gibson, "that just keeps coming up. But nobody knows a thing about them. Who the hell are they?"

Dr. Gibson adjusted his socks. He too listened for the guard. Satisfied, we wouldn't be heard, he leaned in at me. "It's the most intricate organization imaginable," he eventually remarked. "Miami knows everything there is to know. I have been in the intelligence business all my life and this is the next evolution."

"Are you getting theatrical on me?"

Dr. Gibson cracked his knuckles. He peered at me and kept his voice low. "My good man, Miami is unprecedented," he said. "It's nature's way of combating the folly of men. I just don't know if Miami will be strong enough to fight physics."

* * *

I learned years ago physics is absolutely neutral, but there's a certain beauty in neutrality and in knowing the inviolable. We are all physics. Everything springs from physics and eventually physics has its way with this world as it does in every world. Physics rules the universe and would certainly have a say in the crisis at hand, and I had to admit I was curious what the great sage of Oxford thought about this most unbending of disciplines.

Dr. Gibson sipped his tea and organized his thoughts. His brilliant mind cut right to my hope.

"The most important aspects of physics in the quest for human harmony are the first and second laws of thermodynamics," Dr. Gibson began, "as they most aptly describe the fundamental action of the universe."

"I know these laws, but give me your take on them."

Dr. Gibson drew in a breath. He seemed pleased I knew the laws. "Well, the first law is that the total energy of the universe is constant and although energy can be exchanged it is impossible to create or destroy," he said.

"What about the second law?"

"The amount of energy available for work is always decreasing as exchanges of energy produce waste heat that can't be regained. This is known as entropy."

"Entropy is universal."

"Absolutely, my good man, and the two laws taken together mandate the universe is winding down."

"Deteriorating?"

"Yes, entropy is the tendency of systems to break down, to move toward greater confusion and disorder with the passage of time. Eventually, we run out of any energy available for work, known as the 'heat death' of the universe."

"No energy and thus no motion or life."

"That's very well put. But more immediately, and more to our purposes, entropy proves that *all systems trend toward chaos,* including the system of international relations and human affairs."

"You're saying physics predicted the current global crisis was bound to happen?"

The old gentleman smiled at me. "Well, let me show you how it might be possible," he said, rubbing his stubble. "Remember, prediction is always a dangerous game, but clearly we are trending toward chaos."

"And the tendency toward chaos provides a temporal direction known as the 'arrow of time' just as Einstein formulated."

Dr. Gibson was astounded. "By God man, that's mighty impressive," he said in delight. "Perhaps you should be giving the lecture."

I smiled at him. "No, I'll pass thank you, but the second law of thermodynamics sets the limits we are forced to live with; we cannot reverse time or entropy and every action we take either accelerates or decelerates the entropic process."

Dr. Gibson sat up. "Fine way to put it, absolutely, we determine how quickly or slowly the available energy in the world is dissipated," he noted. "But the trend is always toward an exhaustion of energy, toward entropy."

I shook my head. "No, wait just a second, some argue that through the passage of time the world is becoming more ordered and not as chaotic. Ilya Prigogine won a Nobel Prize for that belief."

Dr. Gibson looked at me suspiciously, but admiringly. "Yes," he said, "but that would be both right and wrong. When we increase order, we accelerate entropy. That's inevitable. You're goading me, Colonist."

"No, just leading you to a resolution of the current crisis, I hope."

Dr. Gibson shrugged his shoulders. "Fine, we're ordering the world, but that ordering comes at a cost, a cost of increasing overall chaos" he said. "And now we have harnessed the power of the sun."

I made the linkage of the sun to nuclear weaponry, as the sun is a constantly exploding hydrogen bomb and thus a nuclear weapon is a mini sun. From there, I went to the current global crisis.

"So perhaps we've ordered the world with nuclear technology but seen the disorder manifest itself as nuclear weaponry dissipated to multiple countries," I suggested. "That follows the formulations of the laws of thermodynamics."

"Not much of a stretch, is it?" Dr. Gibson said, one eyebrow upraised on his face, searching me for confirmation. "And until recently we've also ordered the world economically, but now we know this ordering has accelerated the rate of eventual chaos as well. We are ruining our planet, our only home, with environmental destruction. Moreover, this current crisis has shattered international trade and business."

I said nothing, weighing his words. His argument made complete sense. The world was indeed ordering itself into its own physical death. Then Dr. Gibson delivered the coup de grace.

"Remember too," he said, "entropy proves the direction of time. *In the case of nuclear weapons, we may literally be running out of time.*"

I sat cogitating. Earth was not the first hospitable planet with intelligent life to order its own demise. I guess you could blame physics. That's why The Council often intervened to save planets from themselves. Even advanced species like The Council recognize the inviolability of entropy; and that recognition is a primary reason we work so hard with other intelligences to someday devise a solution to a universe otherwise proceeding toward its own death. I doubted Dr. Gibson had a human solution to entropy, but the galaxy is full of surprises.

Dr. Gibson took my silence as an opportunity to say more.

"My good man, I once wrote a piece for the Journal of Sociobiology called 'Sociological Implications of the Natural Universe' and it caused quite a stir," he said nostalgically. "Essentially, the piece stated our greatest threat is evolution itself."

"Dr. Stavenen called this the survival drive. She said it ensures human destruction."

"I'm sure she did, but she probably failed to mention the reason is because the survival drive accelerates entropy. As we advance ourselves, we burn energy."

"I can see that. But no species intentionally stops advancing."

"No, and they never will. And that portends much for our discussion of the current global crisis."

"How so?" I asked.

Dr. Gibson rubbed his eyes while he recalled something from his mind. When he found it, he resumed. "Well, part two of my paper concerned entropy and international relations," he stated. "Evolution increases complexity, and carrying our conversation forward this predicts that nations and civilizations face increasingly complex issues."

"That should give us more options at our disposal."

"On the contrary, sport. Complexity has only ensured us more difference of opinion. Difference of opinion is energy and it has led, as entropy would predict, to its own form of chaos, irresolution. And one day, perhaps sooner than we might imagine, entropy may take the form of thermonuclear warfare to end us entirely."

An eerie silence descended upon the room. Outside the closed office door I heard a guard speak to another guard and then be replaced by what I assumed to be another officer. Dr. Gibson relaxed serenely, strangely so, his arms folded loosely across his portly stomach and his eyes drooping from a satisfying breakfast and the relaxing warmth of the room. I had to ask him how he could be so unwound after his last comment.

"Dr. Gibson, how the hell can you be so at peace after what you just said?"

Dr. Gibson blinked his eyes and sat up straight. He unfolded his arms. "I'm a physicist. Physics is its own actor, the lead actor in the play. Entropy is real, as real as anything gets. We physicists expect the world to disintegrate in time."

"Still, preserving the world warrants an effort."

"And as I promised you, my theory has incredible bearing on your assignment. We'll get to that."

I sighed, discouraged. The once savory air seemed dank. "Forgive me, but I'm frustrated with your findings thus far," I said.

Dr. Gibson relaxed again in his chair. He smiled at me. "No harm done, but 'Unison Theory' says much about the failure of international relations. See if you can guess how."

That was an easy one. "The world has become too complex for man to solve his own problems?"

"And do you know why that is?"

I wrote down a note to myself. "The human brain is not capable of deciphering such complexity," I said, reading my note out loud to him. I looked up to find Dr. Gibson practically jumping from his chair.

"My God, you're a fine chap," Dr. Gibson exclaimed, settling back down on his haunches, his eyes sparkling in delight. "You really are, especially for a businessman. Now go on, work yourself into a gibbering lather."

That was an invitation to speculate, although knowing what I know it wasn't truly speculation. It was more of a dissertation.

"The rate of complexity has surpassed man's ability to surmount the problems caused by said complexity," I stated, thoughts cascading in my mind. "Chaos is reigning supreme because man lacks the intelligence to order his world away from his problems. I suppose—"

"That's entropy. What Unison Theory showed was that man is insufficiently evolved to handle the complexity unleashed by the modern world. Man needs to make a quantum jump in brainpower or lower the level of complexity in order to survive. And here's the rub: it's doubtful he'll be able to do either in time to save himself from himself."

I felt suddenly exasperated. "Why the hell did you call it Unison Theory? It should be Discord Theory or some other regrettable name."

Dr. Gibson had anticipated my response. He gawped at me like an executioner. "Because my research and the theory proved my original hypothesis," he said unemotionally, without a hint of trepidation or regret. "I was not out to see if man can unify himself, but rather to test whether complexity ensures entropy, in a causal and reciprocal manner. The mathematical formulae prove its truth. Therefore, unison is achieved, between complexity and our eventual destruction, also known as entropy."

"So GATDP and China's attempted hegemony are testament to human madness?"

"No, my good man, to insufficient brainpower. And that is not the same as madness. These are reasonable men and women in power, but their minds cannot transcend entropy."

"You know of the Triune Brain?"

Dr. Gibson seemed surprised. "Yes, but we won't evolve our way out of our reptilian root during the term of this crisis," he said. "We probably never will; hell, it is people we're talking about here."

"Humans might, if given enough time. They just need to get there."

"Ninety-nine percent of species go extinct, that's entropy."

I stared at the floor before I looked up. I was frustrated. "That's just plain dark," I said, shaking my head at him. "I have to admit—I expected more from you than such a dire prognosis."

"Dark and real," Dr. Gibson said almost robotically, all jovialness vanished like a ghost. "I told you, physics eventually wins. And entropy is the greatest physical law we have."

"You do know that all sentient beings are made up of physics, don't you?" I was hoping he would make the connection that all sentient beings need to work together to reverse entropy. "One cannot separate living physics from material physics, as we all come from the same soup."

Dr. Gibson ground his teeth and placed his hands around his mouth in a classic megaphone position. He wanted to make sure I got his next point.

"Exactly, my good man. Humans are physics personified, subject to the same laws as the material physics which govern the universe. If there are other intelligences out there, they are subject too. It's all about energy states, and humans trend toward chaos and demise as do all energy systems that eventually run down and pass into history. So would any other beings. We can't escape our physics. We can't escape entropy."

I had to interject again. "You know, maybe an intelligent species out there has reordered their brains," I said, showing no respect to my secret, "so as to survive and manage their self-destructive tendencies. Maybe they can't altogether stop the entropic process, but they can sure as hell slow it down. Ever thought of that?"

"Damn, you Americans are an optimistic bunch." Dr. Gibson smirked at me. "You had your bloody revolution and what did that get you?"

"Freedom, and please answer my question."

Dr. Gibson feared I might be growing impatient. He seemed to back up a bit. "Want some tea? Tea can calm the soul."

"No."

I wanted to tell him exactly what I knew. He needed to hear it. I started to speak, against my directives, but one of the guards knocked on the door.

"Come in," Dr. Gibson commanded.

"I hate to bother you sir, but you are needed by the Foreign Office," the guard said, motioning for another guard to act as escort. "We've had a national security breach."

"How long do the ninnies want me this time?"

"You'll be required for two days. We are sorry, sir."

Dr. Gibson rose slowly and I rose with him. He extended his hand. "I apologize for having to cut this short," he said, "but Her Majesty owns me. I am recommending you on to Dr. Faro. See what she has to say."

I shook his hand goodbye. Another guard motioned for me to exit immediately, which I did. The interview was over and I was no closer to a solution. I hadn't hoped Dr. Gibson had a way out of entropy; finer minds in other worlds have tried with no success. But I had wished he had a recommendation to slow it all down, at least on Earth, starting with the current crisis. I wanted diffusion. I got accretion. When I walked into the open air of Oxford only then did I realize how much entropy had smacked me directly in the face. The human future might indeed be winding down. This current geopolitical crisis proved just as much. Although a pretty day outside, the world seemed an empty iron cage and to lift me I thought of Jenny and the time I would spend with her.

NINE

Reuters—New Delhi, India

September 9, 2017

The government here today remained conspicuously silent regarding widespread reports of unidentified flying objects (UFOs) over the capital city here late last evening. Correspondents in Beijing, Kuala Lumpur, Shanghai, Karachi, Tokyo, Singapore, and Manila have reported similar waves of sightings in the past few days. In Karachi alone, witnesses reported seeing hundreds of disk-shaped lights dance in and out of the clouds, some hovering for minutes before finally darting away.

In a related story, the Brazilian government confirmed an aerial object crashed eighty-nine miles east of Sao Paulo after a wave of UFO sightings stretching from the Atlantic Ocean to the interior of the country occurred late last week. So far, there have been no official reports of the size or nature of the object.

Reports of UFOs in the skies above San Francisco, Miami, Boston, and Portland are as yet unconfirmed.

I had breakfast in London the next morning in an Internet café jammed with junior suits and tourists with heavy accents. Headline reports of war and UFO sightings were everywhere and Nicholas was front page news. Sitting down, I ate my cinnamon bread next to a pleasant Englishman named Peter who insisted I venture to Wimbledon one day because tennis was England's grandest sport. He was a truly friendly sort and so we commiserated about royalty, the state of the economy, the sad shape of British theater, and finally about American icons misbehaving all over Europe until the morning shattered like dropped crystal from a watchtower.

The screams coming from the television at first seemed far away and certainly surreal: a chemical attack in a Parisian soccer stadium by a group of Muslim extremists from Pakistan caused 25,000 dead in a matter of minutes, the death toll sure to rise and the authorities helpless to do much of anything about it. Seems France had recently sided with India in the Kashmiri dispute and French citizenry had paid the price. Everyone in the café sat glued to the television; hands went to mouths and shoulders slumped. I heard the first sobs two tables over. A watery channel away Paris witnessed a gruesome clash of wills, as sirens wailed and bodies mounted and rescuers choked to death in the chemical haze of an embarrassed morning sun. If I never remember anything else from that café, it was the face of every patron, eyes frozen and petrified, like a rime fossil uncovered in stratums and stratums of upland snow.

The world was indeed ripping apart. There seemed no way to stop it.

I pulled my laptop from its case, ran out the door, found a nearby bench, and saw that Jenny had e-mailed me with our agenda for the day. I grabbed some water from a street stand before heading over to meet Jenny at the world famous Kensington Gardens.

As the news spread, the streets turned to ice.

"My God, can you believe it?" a woman yelled, as she ran by. She was crying so hard she nearly fell over.

"Who would do this?" another woman bawled, running from the other direction.

I tried to assist her, but she was gone in a flash. All around me, people sought explanation, but there wasn't any. Nothing made any sense. I walked for awhile until a stranger staggered toward me.

"What is happening to this world?" the man screamed, tucking his child into his arms. His wife was so shaken she had to sit down.

"I don't know," I responded, as the man cradled his wife, "I wish I could help."

Life that morning had entered into hell. For all his creative powers, mankind seemed powerless to reign in his darker side, and in the battle for his very soul he was indeed losing his very mind.

I scoured for Jenny while the world held its breath, walking The Round Pond three times before Jenny finally came running toward me, her face puffy about the eyes.

"I can't believe it," she gasped inside my arms. Muffled, I heard her utter "those poor people are all dead."

I felt the softness of her hug. I felt her warmth and fullness. The feeling went so far within me I had to push away.

"You're not going to China," I said, commanding her. "The world is crazy right now."

Jenny reached up and kissed me softly on the lips. "I have to go to China," she said, wiping tears away from her cheeks. "It's the opportunity of a lifetime. Timing is everything and this is my big career break. Plus, I need the money."

"I'll pay you not to go."

Jenny poured herself into my arms again. "Just hug me," she said, burying her head into my chest.

I did as directed and pulled her close to me. Jenny nuzzled around me like a loving cat.

"I love you," she whispered up at me. "I love you so very much."

* * *

We walked hand in hand in a long silence toward the Italian Gardens when finally Jenny started talking of her assignment in China.

"Michel, my boss, and I must make a decision regarding some new information."

"What information?" I asked.

"You're sworn to secrecy."

"Yeah sure."

"I mean it David."

"I promise."

Jenny took both of my hands into hers. "I need your insights," she said, scanning my sincerity. "Remember when I told you Sharon is friends with Tietnan, the daughter of Mien Jinkao, the Chinese democratic reformer?"

"Yes, that's a great connection."

"And that Tietnan is arranging an interview for me with her mother?"

"Of course I do. That's why you're going to China."

Jenny straightened her collar. "Well, Mien Jinkao has a contact high in the Chinese military, a closet democrat himself, who informed Mien Jinkao that China is encouraging Pakistan to provide The Islamic State with a nuclear weapon," she said.

"What? That sounds crazy."

"I know, but Michel and I believe Tietnan, on instructions from her mother, is trying to let us know the only way she can."

"Because her mother has no direct proof and can't divulge her source without compromising her informant?"

Jenny nodded. "Yes, but Michel thinks I can get more out of her in person. So what do we do about it?"

I was dubious. "I need to hear more. There has to be a rationale for that scenario, some ultimate goal."

"Okay, then try this on for size. The Chinese want retribution for the United States originating GATDP and stirring antagonisms. GATDP is designed to contain the Chinese and they won't stand for it. China figured Taiwan was theirs anyway, but they weren't sure if America would honor their longstanding treaty with the Taiwanese. I mean, America hasn't done much yet, but we still might do something."

"Sounds logical so far."

"Well, China believes a nuclear terrorist attack on American soil would preoccupy America with Muslim extremism and therefore President

Rice will cede Taiwan to the Chinese. Taiwan is lost anyway, although the Chinese are concerned we may retaliate. In China's eyes, it's worth the gamble."

I was still skeptical. "Good in theory, but China needs America to be economically viable and a vaporized American city would not only decimate the United States, but the world economy as well."

Jenny perked up. She had awaited my exact comment.

"Then listen to this," she said excitedly. "A terrorist nuclear attack on American soil promulgated by China and Pakistan puts India on the defensive because it shows Pakistan's willingness to use its nuclear arsenal for first strikes. That's a new development."

"Yes, a game changer, but a long shot at best."

Jenny was undeterred. "Tietnan said if India were to attack Pakistan preemptively, India could expect the Muslim world to rally around Pakistan and thereby lure the entire Middle East into the Pakistani and Chinese camp," she said. "China will have the relations to control the oil supply it so desperately craves."

"Forget India, if the United States proves the bomb came from Pakistan then America will vaporize Pakistan unilaterally, without India being involved."

Jenny shook her head no. "Would they, with China as Pakistan's benefactor and protector?" she asked. "Aren't we then talking about World War III?"

It was obvious somebody had thought this whole scenario out fairly well. That worried me more than the specifics.

"Still," I protested, "the global economic fallout, no pun intended, of a vaporized American city is calamitous for China."

"Fine, but listen to this; Tietnan also mentioned that China surmises a short-term global economic meltdown is worth securing an oil supply for the next hundred years through their dominant relationship in the Middle East. If the vaporized American city is New York, then China also becomes the world's primary banker. Her source also said extremists may launch a major terrorist attack against American interests somewhere in the Far East in a matter of days. I have to talk to Mien Jinkao to see what she knows."

Nicholas once told me supreme power rests with the world's primary banker. It was eerie Jenny had used that exact wording. And New York wouldn't have to be the city hit. A nuclear attack on any American city would do, as the world's money would flow out of the United States and into China like a giant tsunami.

"Okay, maybe there's some credence to your theory, but remember when I told you there are worse things than a nuclear war?" I asked her.

Jenny recalled our previous conversation. "Sure, how a species can lose its innocence or something. I didn't understand it then and I don't understand it now."

I drew in a big breath. "Events are spiraling out of control," I said. "With each passing day a new complication arises and with each new complication the global crisis gets wrapped tighter than a wad of micro fiber. Soon, it will be impossible to unravel. The loss of innocence will follow."

"Are you saying a nuclear war is inevitable?"

I glanced away and then back at Jenny. "No, I'm not saying that at all," I said, debating whether to offer a further explanation. My directives were flashing at me like neon signs.

Confused, Jenny asked her next question anyway. "Okay, I give up, what stops a nuclear war if events lead us inexorably toward Armageddon?"

I paused. The neon signs quit flashing. But I almost choked on the word that followed. "Intervention," I finally muttered, "and the loss of innocence will follow immediately."

Jenny looked as though she had seen a ghost. "Intervention? What kind of intervention are you talking about?"

I went further. "You heard about the sightings reports from New Delhi and from Brazil?"

I saw goose bumps appear on Jenny's arms. Her jaw dropped, as she scrutinized everything about me. "The UFOs," she said, "they'll intervene if they have to, is that it?"

I cleared my throat. I couldn't believe how much I trusted her.

"There isn't a government in the world that knows their true intentions," I said. "The UFO presence is a mystery, one that humanity is not yet prepared to accept, but my clearance has allowed me to know governments are aware of their presence."

"My God, are there beings that will intervene to save us? Are we really there?"

I held Jenny to me. "Yes, we are," I whispered in her ear. "But they are more concerned with saving the planet, not necessarily with saving human life."

Tears formed again in Jenny's eyes. It had been an emotional morning. "We should be worried, shouldn't we?" she asked, trembling.

"Humanity should be very worried."

I should have said *we*. Jenny caught it. For a slight second, she retreated. I don't know much about love and trust, but I learned something of it just then.

"I don't care what you are," Jenny said, her eyes filled with tenderness, her full caress returning. "I love you and I always will. You're the most wonderful thing that ever happened to me."

I pulled Jenny closer. We kissed as passionately as we had ever kissed.

"Please don't go to China," I pleaded with her. "Flights are about to be suspended anyway. The entire country is about to be closed off from any travel."

"I have to go. Promise you'll miss me."

"With everything I have."

Separating felt like my insides were being ripped out, so I couldn't let her go. We must have hugged for five minutes straight. Somehow, whatever we were feeling overcame the news of the day.

When Jenny finally backed away a step, I looked down at the biggest grin I had ever seen in my life. "I knew we would get this close," she said, "I knew we would." Jenny smiled well into the night and when I finally watched her board her flight to China at London's Heathrow Airport only then did I quit smiling myself. An hour later I received an email from Manuela Faro requesting I come alone and visit her river retreat on the Iguaza River. So I caught a flight to Buenos Aires, but never could have I imagined what I was about to hear.

TEN

Associated Press—Berlin, Germany
September 11, 2017
Prime Minister Gerhard Wilboken issued an impassioned plea this morning for the leaders of the G-7 nations, GATDP, Russia, China, North Korea, and Pakistan to convene immediately at his personal hideaway near Munich, Bavaria in what analysts here are calling a "global summit." His invitation also extended to the leaders of Saudi Arabia, Iran, Egypt, Israel, Brazil, and South Africa. Wilboken, perhaps the most moderating voice in the world today, has called the current global crisis "our Archduke Ferdinand and our own Manchuria. If we don't stop this senselessness now, we will enter a time of a thousand mushroom clouds and none of us will live long enough to name it World War III." Privately, government officials here are doubtful Wilboken's plea will be heeded.

The weather coming into Buenos Aires was turbulent and the airliner bounced like a rubber ball over the runway at Ezeiza International airport; we momentarily lost power and the left wing scraped the ground because of the brief power outage. For a moment I figured we were all dead. I hate flying. Too many things can go wrong. I thought of the irony of Jenny flying into possibly the most dangerous country in the world, China, while I might be crash landing in one of the safest, Argentina. The man seated to my left, a Portenos businessman and a wonderful conversationalist, stood up and glanced down at me when we arrived at the gate.

"I told you we'd make it," he said smiling.

"Yeah, but I'm fifty years older," I complained. "I thought this junk heap would come apart."

The businessman patted my shoulder. "Enjoy this city, the prettiest in South America," he said graciously.

"I hope he lives to appreciate it," another man said, turning to face us, standing one row ahead in the aisle and obviously listening in. "Japan conducted her first nuclear test today and now the Chinese are furious."

The businessman gave a look of agreement. "A nuclear armed Japan incites the worst historical antagonisms in China," he said to the man.

"Yes, sorry to eavesdrop, but earlier while you two were chatting, Prime Minister Nakashima stated Japan has enough nuclear weapons to destroy any regional belligerent. China immediately declared war."

The man's wife pulled him forward down the aisle. Chagrined, he made his way toward an exit.

The Portenos businessman found another thought. "At least there is a ground stalemate in Kashmir. Neither the Indians nor the Pakistanis are winning. But it's hard to believe Taiwan is fully occupied; the world has indeed changed."

"Yes, it has."

"In any case, enjoy your stay. You'll be safe here."

The man grabbed his carry on bag and made his way toward the front of the plane. I watched him disappear behind a mob of people.

So I went about my business. I walked for awhile and must have looked particularly inept.

"Are you lost?" a pretty voice asked me. I turned to face her. She couldn't have been much over twenty five, but she wore airport security blue and looked official.

"Just checking for a restaurant," I replied.

"Over there," she said, pointing to my left.

I saw an eatery, small but adequate. "Thanks, and by the way your English is excellent," I said, complimenting her wonderful pronunciation. She seemed almost fluent.

The young woman blushed. "Thank you, but I think I studied the wrong language in school. Soon we'll all be speaking Chinese."

"Why do you say that?"

The young woman caught herself. "That's right, your flight was trans-continental so you haven't heard the latest news."

"Heard what?"

The young woman straightened her uniform. "China and North Korea just invaded South Korea and South Korea is falling fast," she said glumly. "The Japanese are trying to help....... but with little success."

"No?"

"Yes, we have suspended all flights between here and Asia."

Before I could ask her what else she knew, she scooted away to help another confused passenger.

I walked into the eatery as a small crowd stood in front of a hanging television. "The world is at war," a man lamented, turning to his friend. "I guess we were due for another one. I thought Hitler would be the last."

"We will be lucky to survive it," said his friend. "At least the Nazis didn't have nuclear weapons."

Slowly, the crowd dissipated. After what can only be described as a tostada with some sort of cake bread, I gathered my luggage and made my way up to the concourse, waiting for my ride to the river retreat. Manuela Faro left me a message indicating a chauffer would come at precisely twelve noon and that after a short drive through Buenos Aires we would helicopter up the Iguaza River.

Within minutes, a stout middle aged man with a crisp moustache approached me with a handshake and an engaging smile.

"Mr. Jordan, I am Enrique Socorro, Manuela's personal assistant and bodyguard. Please, come with me."

"Have we met?" I asked the man.

"No, but your face is very recognizable and readily available on the Internet because of your global fund raising efforts. Now please, we haven't much time."

The man made his way with my luggage to a parked Mercedes sedan on the left side of the concourse road. I followed him. He opened the trunk and placed my bags in hastily.

"Please, do not delay, Mr. Jordan," he shouted, as he made his way around the far side of the car. "Time is of the essence."

The passenger door unlocked and I climbed into the vehicle. We sped away from the curb, swerving repeatedly through bumper traffic exiting the airport, until we cleared the concourse. I waited for the proper moment to speak.

"How long is the drive?"

"Oh, no more than an hour. We will have ample opportunity to talk. Unfortunately, we shall only glimpse the city while passing."

"Yes, this is no time for tourism. I just heard South Korea is falling."

The man sighed. "No one knew the strength of the Chinese army. The Chinese also unleashed a ground assault an hour ago through Laos and Myanmar against Thailand, with permission from both countries, as the Chinese claim to be securing their borders."

"Well, I heard Buenos Aires—"

The man ignored my comment and interrupted me. "Under the seat, you will find an agenda. Study it now, please."

I reached under the seat and felt a single sheet of paper. I pulled it up and glanced at it. On the paper were typed the words: *Greet, Eat, Appreciate, Situate.*

I knew the author. Manuela Faro was known for brevity and clarity. My chauffeur steered our car onto the major highway leading into the city, beginning our conversation with a fascinating account of Argentine history and Argentina's role in geopolitical relations. We were up to the

Falkland Islands War of 1982 when I noticed the gleaming towers of downtown Buenos Aires fast approaching on my right. I felt a momentary and marvelous appreciation for the Old World, a world now precariously fading into the horrors of the modern age, replete with missiles and guns and tanks and other inexcusable hatred for one another.

*   *   *

My stomach however was doing cartwheels from the stress of transcontinental flight and a mushy airport tostada; Mr. Socorro must have noticed my suffering because he gave me an antacid tablet and an icy bottle of water to sip while we drove onward. The highway meandered until it passed directly to the side of Argentina's capital city.

"Okay, this will be your one look into the city," Mr. Socorro said.

I turned and looked out my side window.

"See the texture and richness in her pattern? One feels Buenos Aires in the hands."

We came to a stop in the highway. I rolled the window down and listened.

"Hear that?" Mr. Socorro questioned me.

"Yes, she strums like a seductive guitar."

The man nodded. He gazed at the city like a poet in love. "A temptress lying easily in your arms," he cadenced, "her velvety embrace obsessing any man. If a city can be a beautiful woman, that city is Buenos Aires."

"Something tells me you loved a woman here."

The man nodded again and smiled. "Yes, once. It was grand. But make no mistake, Mr. Jordan, losing the woman you love, can hurt you like nothing else in this world."

To my disappointment the highway wove again, this time out of the woman's caress and into the outskirts. We passed some ramshackle neighborhoods, barrios really, and then we turned down a choppy road that wandered back up a gentle hill and stopped. A helicopter waited on a helipad. The rotors were off and the pilot climbed out from the cockpit and opened our doors.

"Good afternoon, Mr. Jordan," the pilot said, greeting me. "I am Manuela Faro's personal pilot, Blake Freeman. I'm an American like you."

"Nice to meet you.

Enrique Socorro hustled to get my luggage from the trunk of the car. "Mr. Socorro won't be joining us, but I trust you had a pleasant conversation," the pilot said to me.

"Yes, Mr. Socorro was plenty informative. I think he actually warmed to me after the first few minutes."

Mr. Socorro took my luggage and loaded it into the back compartment of the helicopter. "That would make you the first," the pilot said to me, under his breath. "But he is the best at what he does. The government here would not mind if Manuela were dead."

His comment surprised me. "So you are more than Manuela's pilot, you are a confidant?" I asked him.

The pilot did not change expression. "Yes, you might say that. So is Mr. Socorro; he's in charge of her security. And soon, you will be Dr. Faro's confidant as well."

I said nothing, but the pilot looked me over. "I understand you're not a good flier," he said, his face quizzing me. "I must warn you; the air currents over the Iguaza are tricky. We'll experience hair raising dips and dives. But the scenery is magnificent."

I felt my stomach tighten. "Superb," I said sardonically, "just what I needed to hear."

Mr. Freeman smiled again. "I'll fly us water top over the river and tight on the falls," he said, using his hand to simulate the helicopter. "Like I said, the scenery is a postcard. I never grow tired of it."

I gulped hard. "Just get me there as you see me now."

"Soiling your pants?" Mr. Socorro said, laughing to the pilot, as he caught the last bit of our conversation. "That should be easy enough."

He then turned to me. "Mr. Freeman can accommodate you, I'm sure," he said, still laughing, extending his hand toward mine for a handshake. "It was a pleasure meeting you, sir."

"Likewise," I said, shaking his hand farewell. My hand nearly slid off his grip from the nerves in my stomach. "And thank you for the history lesson; wish me and my pants luck."

*   *   *

I had never been in a helicopter before, but we were in the air before I had a chance to be afraid. Soon, we were straight over the Iguaza. We dove into bladed rain, the clouds swarming like ravens, the downpour at first pelting us and then thumping the windshield like gunfire. I thought the glass might shatter. But Mr. Freeman soon lifted us into a grayish white cloud and then even higher into bright blue sunshine. I looked below. The Iguaza moves so powerfully the earth crumbled at its banks, the air so heavy our rotors chopped like sushi knives. Islands of dirt twirled currents into little spinning avocadoes and then the river went eerily wild.

"You okay?" Mr. Freeman yelled over to me.

"It's stunning. It's just incredible."

I saw him scan ahead. "The worst is over, but that was some squall."

"Too much beauty to be sick," I hollered back

I don't know if Mr. Freeman heard me. We ventured further together in awestruck silence.

As we traveled northward, I gradually noticed the river beginning to calm. Mr. Freeman pointed to a large tributary on my right and as he veered the helicopter up its course I noticed the trees growing taller and thickening in color. What was apple green and dull was now forest green and glossy and what was angry about the river had quieted into exhausted serenity. On the horizon I saw low puffy white clouds without any rain.

"The river is changing now," I commented.

Mr. Freeman faced forward and said nothing; he was too busy steering us through the trees as we descended and followed the tributary's course upstream. Ahead, the river grew narrower and deeper. Amazingly, the water was turquoise and navy with splotches of gold and also glassy clear; never have I seen such water. Usually, bodies of water have different colored sections and blending in the tones leading to another color, but here the colors were mixed together as a mosaic. All four colors would show in a handful of water. Mr. Freeman hovered the helicopter and leaned over toward me.

"You are noticing the water?" he asked me.

"Yes, all of these beautiful colors all at once. How is this possible?"

"The river bottom is limestone and an unusual mix of volcanic pebbles and rare plant life that grows loosely on the stone. Manuela picked this location for its beauty."

"Astonishing," was all I managed.

We came to a large clearing on the left. Behind a few straggler trees sat a large plantation style house, creamy yellow in color, and two guest houses, guarding the plantation home like sentries. A creek flowed where the clearing met the forest darkness.

We had arrived.

Mr. Freeman landed the helicopter in the middle of the clearing and shut off the rotors. Unbuckling, I noticed a tall, angular woman with boysenberry hair stepping gracefully from her home and then pausing on the painted wooden planks of the wraparound front porch, eyeing me. She gradually made her way over to the helicopter. As she came forward, I saw her world famous elegance arrive well before her steps; although over sixty, she was incredibly statuesque, like a bronzed monument come to life, her skin smoother than mocha and her eyelashes like those of a fire dancer. She wore a necklace of turquoise eagles and a golden antelope lounging blithely under a sprawling shade tree.

I stepped from the helicopter to greet her.

"I am so glad you've arrived safely, Mr. Jordan," Manuela said to me. "I understand flying is not your forte."

She gave me a hug. "Mr. Freeman and the Iguaza kept me fully occupied," I said, releasing her. "What a river. I've never seen anything like her."

"Well then, welcome Mr. Jordan. I have played hostess to only three people here: Don Basson, the classical pianist; Carmen Longley, the president of Princeton; and now you. The first two are my dearest friends in life and I have high hopes for you. We will have much to talk about, and I am optimistic it will be much less quarrelsome than our previous phone conversation."

Manuela Faro led me to her plantation manor. Behind me, servants grabbed my belongings. I smelled a fresh pot of coffee brewing as I entered through a swinging teak door and waited for instructions.

"Let's go into my study, Mr. Jordan." We walked past a grand room with a large swirling fan over a dining table and dark rattan chairs. Off to the back right was a study with inlaid teakwood bookshelves, opposing leather couches, and a giant encased well lit map of the world on the primary wall ahead of me. "Please have a seat," Manuela said, gesturing toward the nearest couch.

I took my seat. Outside the river flowed as gently as molasses; I saw it through a huge windowed wall, the jungle crawling into the room. Another servant brought in a serving tray with a silver coffee pot and served us coffee and cream. I hesitated to drink mine, but Manuela spoke to me reassuringly.

"The coffee is decaffeinated, Mr. Jordan," she said, lifting her cup, "we do our homework here."

I grinned at her. "Thank you for considering my needs," I said. The eclecticism of her tastes wasn't lost on me; it was as if the 1960s had merged with Casablanca and the House of Stuart.

We sat in silence. I wondered if she knew of my secrets, curious as to whether so fine a mind could know the unknowable. She said nothing to me and instead waited for her servant to attend to our comforts.

Eventually, the first servant left the room. Another soon brought in a tray of sandwiches and gourmet cheeses. "It may surprise you Mr. Jordan that I pay my servants more than Mr. Freeman or Mr. Socorro," she finally said to me, her servant leaving quietly and closing the door.

"Please, call me David," I suggested, relieved there was at last a conversation.

"No, I will call you Mr. Jordan because such formality will impress upon you the urgency of your task. You however may call me Manuela."

"You were saying something about your servants."

I saw a confirmation. "Yes, I pay them more than my top assistants because I want my life to be an example of how to remedy the world's biggest problem."

"And what problem is that?"

Dr. Faro dropped her chin. "Why, wealth inequality, Mr. Jordan. My sources tell me you met with Dr. Stavenen of Berkeley and Robert Allen Gibson of Oxford, no?"

"Yes, I did."

"Well, I'm sure Dr. Stavenen cited the law of scarcity and the biological survival drive forcing us toward unrestrained self-interest, while Dr. Gibson probably associated the decline of civilization to entropy itself, but the key point is that both tacitly approve of the status quo and its inherent inequalities. Stavenen still believes the U.N. can somehow solve this current crisis, but Gibson has thrown up his hands and defaulted to physics, am I right?"

"You are correct."

Manuela pulled at her necklace. "You see, Mr. Jordan, the world is now paying the price for inequality," she said, "and please do not bore me with references to the hierarchical nature of nature itself as a justification for unrestrained inequality; I'm aware there are winners and losers in life and that inequality has run rampant since the first lapping tides."

I remained quiet and observant. Manuela saw I was content to hear more.

"We, Mr. Jordan, are an opportunity squandered," she said, her eyes piercing my soul. "People had the chance to flatten the inequality into a manageable range, where the hierarchies of nature are preserved to propel us forward through evolutionary competition, but where the weakest are no longer trampled on."

"You mean if people at the bottom were made average humanity would gain?"

Manuela lifted her eyes. "Yes, instead of being a burden to society these individuals would contribute and ultimately pay for themselves. Collectively, you see, we'd have a boost instead of a drain."

"Hasn't this been tried? Isn't that the goal of the World Bank and IMF?"

Manuela curled herself on her couch. She grabbed a couch blanket and threw it over her legs. "Tried by whom, Mr. Jordan?" she asked me, ignoring my World Bank and IMF references. "Our elites have fecklessly pursued their self-interest to the ruination of human society. GATDP and the Chinese resistance to the pact are fundamentally caused by leadership that has forsaken the people who give them their very power."

"Explain that linkage for me."

"Okay, it goes something like this: societal elites attempt to boost their nation's standard of living to maintain their own personal power, but only to the extent that their power is maintained, nothing more."

"So elites do the minimum required?"

"Yes, it's the old Roman game of 'bread and circuses,' give your citizenry ample food and sufficient entertainment and you can rule them without magnanimity. But never lift them so much that it changes the game. The World Bank and the IMF are classic examples of trying to lift the world enough to maintain their power without ever really changing things."

"So you've tried to set an example with your own life choices?"

"I have personally chosen to live another way. You've heard of the Chang Society?"

"Sure, the group in Shanghai promoting an egalitarian form of capitalism using 'mutual coercion mutually agreed upon' or something to that effect."

"Not promoted, Mr. Jordan, proved. They raised their weakest members to average members and their companies outperformed the best purely profit driven firms by five to one. Although their highest paid executives made less than their counterparts, they reported higher levels of job satisfaction and personal happiness and their altruism outweighed personal financial gain in every case. They were allowed to excel, but only within a reasonable limit and the collective entity surpassed all expectations."

"I heard there were cultish elements and mind control practices."

Manuela frowned no. "Absolutely not," she said, "that garbage was put forth by the Chinese government. Through meditation, the Chang Society redirected their survival drive, greed if you will, and channeled it into group altruism. They proved it can be done, three million years of human evolution changed in a fortnight. It was remarkable."

If true, this was huge news. "So what happened to them?" I asked.

"They were slaughtered by the Chinese secret police and the cult scandal was the cover story propagated by the government. Once the leadership, including Arthur Chang, was killed, the Society faded away. Unfortunately, we still require leaders."

Through the windows I saw the sky darkening above the river. It seemed a breeze came up and I felt a slight chill in the air. Manuela took a sip of coffee and wrapped her blanket tighter around her legs. I waited again for her to speak.

"As you know, I'm a technologist and a spiritualist," she began. "I started in technology and gravitated toward spiritualism as a sanctuary against the mechanistic worldview of Newton."

That was interesting. She hadn't written about this aspect. "What did you see in technology that made you lose hope?"

Manuela took another sip of coffee. "Well, I observed that technological advancement was destroying us," she said. "The privileged using technology to further their positions increases the likelihood of war; it's like giving bad kids guns."

"I suppose a case can be made."

Manuela scoffed at my comment. "One convincing case, Mr. Jordan," she castigated, unfurling her curl on the couch. "Are you familiar with Hardin's 'Tragedy of the Commons' from 1968?"

"Yes."

"Well, then you know individual self-interest, manifesting as greed, eventually pollutes the system for everyone. Hardin's formulation made him The Chang Society's hero. Nations acting for their own interests produces the same pollution, only on a global scale. Technology is a facilitator in this effluence and globalization is an accelerator."

"What about globalization bringing more of the world together?"

"That's pure hogwash," she said, frowning at me. "The reality of our flattening world is a disparity of thought, not a union of ideas. Globalization has the Chinese and the Americans at each other's throats. We now have race riots on every continent and death camps in over twenty countries."

"So hence spirituality?"

"Yes, I proceeded to spirituality given what I saw. It was a dark time for me, Mr. Jordan, as black as a river night. And remember, I was a chief driver of technological innovation and globally famous for it. I have research labs all over the world, many of which have patented some of the great technological discoveries of our time. Then one day I realized what I was doing—accelerating an inevitable decline."

"And the current global crisis, you feel you helped cause it?"

A look of sadness came over her. "Sure, all of our collective actions over time were leading us to war, but for me, being a leader, I was much guiltier," she said ruefully. "My spiritualism was a reaction against a world gone mad."

"And did spirituality redeem you?"

Manuela's keen eyes grew sharper. She massaged the cup with her hands. "Okay, Mr. Jordan, you asked for it, now it gets extremely interesting."

*   *   *

A river night is eerily transformative. Jungle bugs hummed outside while a breeze stirred the plantation rafters to a song. The moon cast a milky spill on the Iguaza and the jungle breathed with moving life. Things felt natural and aligned. But on Manuela's face was a look of strife.

"Mr. Jordan, you've heard of the Gaia Hypothesis?"

"Yes, the Earth as its own alive being. I was actually just feeling that very thought. "

"And you no doubt know of human will?"

"Of course."

"Well, the intersection of those two is critical to our fate. Human will is much too potent for its own good, overpowering the Gaia with our sickness and greed; so the Gaia as a saving force for itself is impossible. The Earth, for whatever other powers she may possess, will be overrun by human ambition, ravenousness, and our inability to stop our technological progression."

"Then it's up to humans to save themselves from themselves?"

Manuela looked off and then came back to me. "Are you familiar with the work of Teilhard de Chardin?" she asked.

"Yes."

"Well then you know the human story is essentially the evolution of consciousness. People are the product of an amazing saga of evolution, from a primordial sea of single celled organisms, to creatures of ever increasing complexity, to fish and amphibians to land animals, from those to the great apes, and from the great apes to us."

"Yes, humans were the first to achieve consciousness here."

"The only species to do so, Mr. Jordan, and through the single act of consciousness we control the fate of planet Earth. It's up to us."

I couldn't tell her that consciousness is everywhere and is the root of everything. Quantum Mechanics proves as much. But most humans, even the best and brightest, like Dr. Faro herself, still clung to the Newtonian paradigm that consciousness results from brain chemistry and not the grand design of The One. Humans have free will, but the march of consciousness trumps it. So the fate of Earth was actually not up to humans, but rather resided in higher consciousness like The Council and ultimately the Creator. But I had to go along with her line of reasoning, even if I knew it to be false.

"Can man be a benevolent master?" I asked.

I saw in her eyes a look of disdain. "Well hardly Mr. Jordan, for I dare say consider the evidence. Maslow envisioned the human potential movement as a new force in psychology, that through trust, openness, acceptance of self, acceptance of others, and with greater empathy we might change ourselves and build a better world for our children. Yet our collective will manifests itself as pure consumerism, an economic system of accumulation eroding the Earth's natural resources, degrading the environment, alienating the self and condemning most of our members to dreamless futures."

"Sounds bleak."

Manuela rolled her eyes at society. "It's the whole damn political and social spectrum, Mr. Jordan," she said. "And I mean everyone: from communists to Nazis, every religion and philosophy you can name, every culture on Earth, virtually all people everywhere, everyone plays the game of consumerism and wants to grab their fair share of the pie. We're all addicted to comforts and gadgets and owning the latest things. Those at the bottom want the merchandise as much as those at the top; in fact, most revolutionary movements are fundamentally about how to get more stuff. Now, through globalization, we are intensifying an already destructive system. So I can't see us as benevolent stewards of our home, can you?"

"No, I suppose not. Not when you put it that way."

Manuela looked at me dryly. She poured herself another cup of coffee and offered me the same. We both ate sandwiches and cheese for a time.

Then she sat down again. "There's more to the story," she said, tightening her shoulders, "the chapter where I placed my final hopes."

* * *

My recorder was already on, had been on, but I checked it to verify its battery power. I didn't want to miss a word of what came next.

"The failure of the human potential movement to overcome a mechanistic worldview and its resulting consumerist wave gave rise to the hope of spiritual masters," Manuela said, almost in lecture tone. "And the hope was that spiritual masters, including those who had come before us, such as Buddha, Jesus and Gandhi, would pave the way for New Age gurus to unite the peoples of Earth into a common spirituality. But has this happened?"

I thought on her words for a good while. "No, it has only served to divide the world into spiritual camps," I finally said, agreeing to her point. "Far from unity, it has disunited the peoples of this Earth."

"Exactly, Mr. Jordan, and that may be the biggest tragedy of all. Spiritual masters, perhaps inadvertently, have only created more antagonisms in the world, with their followers pitted against other followers for control of human belief. Half the wars on Earth are fought for this very reason."

I thought on her words. There was no unifying spirituality to bind all humans together. I knew this instinctually but I had never made the association in quite the same way, from the evolution of consciousness through to the Newtonian revolution, to the human potential movement as a counter to the mechanistic paradigm reigning on Earth for the last three hundred years, to spiritual masters as the last resort for man's hopes and dreams. And then Manuela put it as succinctly as humanly possible.

"Spirituality became a 'me' activity instead of an 'us' activity. And so the spirit of humanity is divided."

I felt goose bumps on my arms and neck. How can humans possibly be united as one when their very souls are divided in two? Not only do humans compete and fight for limited resources and possess an inadequate brain, but their spiritual essences are alienated as well.

"So what do humans do?" I asked her.

Dr. Faro smoothed her blanket. She looked at me wistfully. "What we need is a unifying philosophy, Mr. Jordan, one that binds us all together as we should be bound," she responded. "I call it *Sentientism*."

I had never heard of Sentientism. And the woman in front of me had certainly never written about it. Not that I knew of anyway. Manuela paused for effect. Seconds seemed as hours to me. I waited for her to say more, but she just sat there like a stone.

"Enough suspense, what the hell is Sentientism?" I finally asked her.

Manuela's eyes twinkled in delight. "Sentientism is the recognition we are only one of many sentient beings in the universe," she said, with pride in her theory. "That will end our anthropocentrism, man at the center of everything, which has been our demise. You see, our anthropocentric worldview has made us selfish."

"Well, it's about time," I muttered, hoping I wasn't heard. Humans were known throughout the galaxy for their unawareness and pomposity. In fact, it was kind of a galactic joke.

Manuela yawned, but her face sparkled. "Yes, it is about time, Mr. Jordan," she said. "See, only when confronted with the existences of other intelligent beings will we unite as one human race and end our many squabbles here on Earth."

She was still missing one vital connection. "Tie Sentientism into technology," I insisted, knowing that technological progression must be managed for the collective good. In short, a species must be united in their management of technology; in worlds where it's not, calamity results.

Manuela sat back and ruminated. I saw the light go on. "Well, to put a divided human spirit in charge of technology only serves to more powerfully divide us from one another," she said, the realization hitting her. "In a nuclear age, our divided spirits may prove fatal to us all."

She was getting there. "Yes, if the human spirit were united technology would never again threaten man," I said, leading her. "In fact, technology would be used to forward man's common interest and man—."

"In one spirit, man would always have the common interest clearly defined. We would avoid wars, especially nuclear wars. Technology would further our common goals and adhere our world community."

I said nothing and this time waited for her to cogitate further. Our brief relationship had shifted. Now I was in charge. But it's always preferable for a species to come to their own discoveries and Dr. Faro was the human being most likely to deduce the proper gleanings. Well, with the possible exception of Miami, whatever that was. So I had high hopes for her. And it hadn't been easy all these years to underperform given my abilities for the sake of maintaining my secrets; sure, I was successful and connected to lots of important people, but primarily so that I could monitor human events at high levels at the behest of The Council and for the benefit of their mission. Now though, with the Earth on the precipice of annihilation, my best efforts could help humans realize their potential. In fact, I was having the conversation that could lead humans where they most needed to go. I felt good about that, and it almost atoned for all those years living a lie.

"So, we still have a global crisis to solve and I don't see how we are any closer than when I arrived," I commented. "Dig deep and find me an answer."

*   *   *

Manuela rose from her seat and dismissed her servants for the evening. When she returned, the house for the first time felt empty and outside the jungle had quieted to a tropical silence. To my surprise, Manuela closed the large double doors of the study and came and sat beside me on my couch. In the amber light of the room she was stunningly beautiful, her facial features nearly flawless; it was easy to see why so many men had dreamed of her and why she had captivated the imaginations of so many sculptors and painters. If Venus, the goddess of love, were to take a human form, it would have been Manuela.

In such a moment, I learned much about myself; the two of us alone, the woman beside me perhaps the most tempting combination of beauty and brains the world had ever seen, me sensing her interest or some form of sexual tension, but instead I thought of Jenny. I missed her so much it hurt inside.

Manuela leaned in toward me. "Mr. Jordan, I want to tell you something I've never told another soul," she said. "Do you see the map on the wall?"

"Yes."

Manuela held the map in her eyes like a mountain climber holds a view from atop a snowy summit. "From the time I was a little girl, I knew the world was mine."

"How do you mean?"

Manuela smiled confidently. "I knew I was destined for greatness," she said, "and that my life would be a test of the maximum human capability. As Gordon Pine of Fox News once said about me, 'I was the reach of man while others were only his grasp.' Or so I thought."

Manuela's look of appreciation fell to a sudden darkness. The primal attraction existing only a moment before had disappeared. What replaced it can only be described as comprehension.

"I understand you're remarkable," I said, truly appreciative, "reading most every word you've written or that was written about you. I know many have considered you humanity's best hope."

Manuela's eyes beheld the map again. "I am a heroine to millions, the most sought after sage since King Solomon himself," she said. "I must keep a wise and confident demeanor, especially in times of crisis. But inside, my soul aches."

"Why? My God, you have done so much with your life."

When a hand slips from another and falls irretrievably into an abyss, well, that look of despair was the look in Manuela's eyes. In her gaze, I knew she felt as far away from her childhood hopes as a woman standing on the far side of the moon.

"I cannot save this world," she said forlornly. "I can't remedy technology gone awry or unite the human spirit into one. GATDP and the Chinese response are simply the latest and scariest example. I have failed and now the world may end because of my failure."

"Wait, you can't quit now. You're needed more than ever."

Startled, Manuela turned to face me as I rose from the couch and started toward the map. She seemed as directionless as a ship in a storm. "You mean I'm needed because of the current crisis?" she finally asked me. "You're wrong, Mr. Jordan, that's up to you and Straka now."

"No, something more pressing," I replied, talking over my shoulder while staring at the map. "I came to see you for another reason besides my mission for Nicholas. Have you heard of Carte Blanche?"

"Sure, bad group of boys. How does that pertain to our discussion?"

I studied the map even closer. "We will get to that shortly," I said. "First though, I read your assessment regarding which cities make the likeliest targets for nuclear terrorism. It was brilliant work."

"You're referring to the NATO study of 2007?"

"Yes."

"That study was classified. How the hell do you know about that analysis?"

"I have my ways."

Manuela was appalled. "NATO leaks like a sieve," she said. "I have been suspicious of them all along. I shouldn't have done any work for NATO because of our ideological differences and what they represent, but Brad Manning interceded. Reluctantly, I said yes."

I had to trust her. Once again, I violated a directive. "Carte Blanche has biological weapons," I said, "and they're close to using them."

Manuela fell back onto the couch. "How many weapons?" she asked me.

"Enough to decimate human life. The weapons still must be placed at their targets, so they are almost guaranteed to be en route. I figure we have at most a day or two."

Dr. Faro stood up, grabbed some water, and rubbed it on her face. She sat back down, pallid. "How can I help?" she finally asked me.

"I need your best effort here, so muster and muster quickly. Look at the map again and tell me what cities will be *biological* weapons targets. The plot places the weapons in cities where that nation retaliates against their natural enemy or where because of wind currents drift is maximized."

"The weapons have signatures?"

"Yes."

"Where did the weapons come from?"

"From the old Soviet stockpile."

"But signatures can't be switched; the canisters will be pinpointed to the Soviet era."

I had to confide in her again. "No, there's a new technology allowing switching of signatures," I said. "Trust me, it's there."

Manuela rubbed her eyes. The magnitude of the situation hit her at exactly that moment. "Mr. Jordan, when you come for a visit, you come for a visit," she said, humorously disdaining. "I feel like beating the shit out of you."

"Yes, I do come for a visit. And don't hit me. The world is at stake, so get this right."

Manuela thought for a time. She peered at the map. "Okay then, South American countries have no natural enemies," she said, beginning to focus.

"Correct."

"So maximum drift for South America is Rio de Janeiro. Wind currents are perfect to cover the largest percentage of the continent."

"Yes, that's my assessment as well. I think the Rio canister will be exceptionally potent. Now give me eight more cities."

Manuela smiled a devious smile. "You're thinking of canister scans," she said knowingly. "The housing of the canisters is treated to safeguard the virus, but that coating can be scanned."

"Yes, with a biometrical oscillator amplified over a city. Best guess is that we're looking for up to 8-9 canisters. But we can only scan ten cities, so we need to be accurate because the oscillators can't be regenerated for at least a month."

Manuela nodded. She took her time staring at the map, then rose to grab a closer look. "Shanghai, Rio de Janeiro, Moscow, Berlin, Chicago, Beirut, New Delhi, Singapore, and Monrovia," she said. "Those are your cities."

"Those match very closely your nuclear cities in your NATO report because of wind currents?"

Manuela took a deep breath. "Yes, but I factored in the signatures and who would retaliate and why," she said.

"I had Tel Aviv instead of Beirut."

Dr. Faro thought for a second. "The drift will be the same for both, covering the Middle East and the northern half of Africa," she said pensively, "but Beirut has much less security than Tel Aviv."

"We have an extra oscillator so we can scan both Beirut and Tel Aviv. The Americans made the machines available to the U.N., just last week."

Manuela's face reddened. My words had done little to comfort her. "My God, what else can go wrong," she said despairingly. "If we select the wrong cities, it's game over."

"Do you want to look at the map again?"

Manuela went to the map and rubbed her right hand over Asia, cogitating. She also peered momentarily at Australia. "No, those are your cities; the wildcard would be Sydney, but they won't waste a weapon whose potency peaks over Antarctica," she said, turning to face me.

I still had one question regarding cities that I had struggled with for hours in my head. I figured this could be the difference maker. Eric Waller would waffle on this one as well, going either way, and although I had studied his thought patterns for years I still had no idea which way his mind would lean. "Did you think of Jakarta instead of Singapore?" I asked Dr. Faro.

Dr. Faro put her hands together in the prayer formation. "I did, it's very close between them, but Singapore has stronger wind currents," she declared. "The drift will cover more distance and move faster than from Jakarta."

I peered over the map one final time. Jakarta had double the population of Singapore, hence more instant deaths, but Manuela's arguments made sense. "Good, those are our cities," I finally concluded. "I hope you're as smart as I think you are, Dr. Faro. And thank you; I needed a second opinion."

Manuela wiggled her fingers nervously. She finally removed her eyes from the map. "My God, I hope you're right," she said, searching me for confirmation. "If we're wrong, millions of people will die."

* * *

The next step was an easy one.

"Do you have a secure land line?" I asked her.

"Yes, Mr. Socorro scans the line daily for interference; it's always clean."

"You trust him?"

"More than I trust you."

I sat back down on the couch. "Fair enough, we will call Nicholas," I said, motioning for Manuela to bring me the phone as I pulled the code numbers for a land line call to Nicholas' number from my cell phone. It was an extra security step, but probably well worth it. Manuela brought the phone and its long cord along with her and sat beside me on the couch.

I dialed Nicholas' extra security code and cell phone number.

"Hello," I heard him answer.

"Nicholas, this is David."

"Oh thank God," Nicholas said. "Tell me you're not still vacationing in South America."

"I'm here with Dr. Faro, so shut up and listen."

There was a pause letting me know Nicholas understood the seriousness of my tone. "Yes David, go on."

"Carte Blanche has biological weapons and they're maybe hours away from using them," I said. "It's a money making scheme to short global stock markets and millions of people will die unless you do as I say."

"Dear God."

With Nicholas under great strain, it was best to get directly to the point. I learned that at Williams years ago.

"The United Nations has ten biometrical oscillators in its global security division, am I right?" I asked him.

"David, how the hell do you know about the oscillators? I barely know myself."

"I just know. Is the number ten?"

"Yes, but how—"

"Good," I said, interrupting him. "Dr. Faro and I have gamed out all possible target cities and we're reasonably sure we have them pegged. We could be wrong on a city or two, but it's the best we can do."

I actually heard Nicholas shake through the line. "David, I am coming unglued here," he screamed at me. "Do you hear me, absolutely unglued? Now I have to fuck with this?"

"Nicholas, calm down. I know each continent has an oscillator so theoretically the oscillators can be placed in less than a day. Have the global security division deliver the oscillators to the cities. Conduct the scans immediately."

"Which cities, David? Are you certain?"

"I will email you the list of cities shortly; and I am as certain as I can be."

"But the scans can only be conducted for a few days; after that, we have to regenerate the oscillators. Are you sure about the time frame?"

"If my calculations are correct, the weapons will be placed in the next day or so. Now I have to go. Good luck."

"David, just wait a fucking minute, just fucking wait," Nicholas shouted hysterically. "I need assurances from you. You can't just call me and lay this crap on me. If you are wrong and I waste the scans, I am out of a job."

"I know Nicholas. Now calm down. Goodnight."

I hung up the phone and emailed the cities list to Nicholas, and took a very satisfied breath. I looked over at Manuela and saw her grimacing at me.

"I hope this little mapping exercise helped you, but the world is still on the brink of nuclear war," she said.

"Oh, you still have a trick in your bag. You have wanted to tell me more since I arrived."

"What? You suppose a lot, Mr. Jordan, and what if it's not enough?"

"Then I will figure something else out."

Manuela raised an eyebrow. "Are you always so confident?" she asked me. "I don't know whether to love or hate you right now, but you are astoundingly self-possessed in crisis. Why the hell aren't you petrified?"

"It's my job to be a little brash. Somebody has to be, especially in this soup. And try being my friend; I could use one of those these days."

Dr. Faro glared at me. She approached me and came near. "Fine, a friend I will be," she said, "and excuse me for being so crass, but you and I should be having sex." My jaw dropped. I didn't know what to say. I suppose I looked like a man who finds his car has been towed. "Oh come now, Mr. Jordan, don't give me that look," Manuela went on. "We have both felt the attraction since the moment you arrived. Crises build tension and we could both benefit from making each other feel good. And I'm still upset about you having that NATO report. You're a surprising man, David Jordan, although quite unsettling."

I had to say something. "Manuela, it's not that I don't find you......
well you know......... it's just that I have a girlfriend and I couldn't hurt
her," I said, clearly stammering. "And don't be upset about the damn report,
I have tons of connections at NATO. And I am flattered you find me surprising; but something tells me you know someone else who surprises you
just as much. I need a name."

Dr. Faro eyed me suspiciously. She seemed slightly scorned. "Well,
you can't blame a girl for trying," she said. "It can get lonely in this jungle.
And yes, Mr. Jordan, the only person who can help you now is Franco
Varese. Mr. Varese lives in Miami, Florida. And he, like you, is an honorable man and as frustrating as hell."

* * *

I had never heard of Franco Varese and was quite sure not many others had either. I know most people of note and his name was exceedingly
unfamiliar. Alas, I had to admit I was curious about him, but since he was
an unknown I couldn't gauge his worth. Besides, Nicholas would never
approve of me meeting this man, especially at a time like this, what with
the world on the verge of nuclear annihilation and the Hellenic taskmaster
already suspicious of my 'vacation' time in South America. But when Dr.
Faro gives you a name, you listen and you listen well.

"A few years back," Manuela began, "I was in Cortina for a conference, having dinner with Anthony Cassini, whom you know through Mr.
Straka."

"I know Cassini well."

"Well, Cassini was the democratic socialist leader in Italy and headed
shortly for Premier. So over antipasti Cassini introduced me to Mr. Varese."

"Was it a spontaneous introduction?"

Manuela lurched back. "Why no, I always felt the encounter was pre-
arranged," she said. "Franco Varese joined us for dinner and the conversation quickly turned to my qualifications and the challenge of managing
world order. The whole gambit was a job interview."

"What kind of job?"

Manuela hesitated. "Well, I'm not sure exactly, but it's the kind of job not listed anywhere," she finally said, "not even in circles that circle solely back to themselves."

"Are you sure?"

"Certain."

Something rustled outside the window. Manuela rose to look outside and then returned to her seat. "It was nothing," she said, referencing her glance to the jungle. She dimmed the light and sat again, coming forward, speaking very softly. "I want to tell you something in the strictest of confidence, Mr. Jordan."

"Sure, I won't say a word."

"I would prefer this not be recorded. And since we are on it, please erase my spurned sexual advance."

We both smiled at each other. I obliged her request and turned off my recorder.

Dr. Faro leaned in again. "I have learned, Mr. Jordan, there are cabals, as stealthy as sables at midnight, and I'm convinced one operates at a supra level," she whispered.

"Is this Franco Varese?"

"I can't prove it, but his trail leads to nowhere."

"Okay, tell me more about him."

Manuela rubbed her forehead. "Well, when I met Varese in Cortina I was working at the intersection of technology and spirit, seeking peak experiences and performance highs, that sort of thing."

"Go on."

"Well, Cassini left the dinner table to take a phone call and I remember Varese was particularly interested in my ongoing work. It was just he and I. He asked lots of questions, comparing my answers with a mental checklist. Three days later while in Rochester, New York, I was visited by an Air Force colonel named Thomas Broderick, who showed me a file on the military's research into this field. Varese must have clued him into my work."

"You're kidding me."

"No, the Air Force had induced test subjects into these transformative states and were basically 'at will' in their procedures. There was integration of brain and soul. It was extraordinary."

"Why did they show you? Were you cleared for that?"

Manuela never hesitated. "Well, Thomas Broderick informed me his superiors were interested in the philosophical implications of these procedures and I was the most qualified person for that analysis. He gave me instructions on the direction of my work and I gave him my report a month later at an elaborately staged drop-off in Sussex County. Two days later my bank account grew by a hundred thousand dollars."

"Come on. That's something out of a bad spy novel."

Manuela snickered at my suggestion. "No Mr. Jordan, what's more amazing is there's no Thomas Broderick," she said, her face brightening. "My people researched for six months and found no such person. Thomas Broderick was a complete dead end."

"Your people had access to military files?"

"Yes, at the level of espionage."

"Was there anything else?"

Manuela swallowed hard. "I believed my work was unsurpassed; yet I was at least a decade behind what was in that file," she said, shaking her head. "I will admit my ego was deflated. But that's not what really bothered me. What bothered me was that Broderick intimated the military was conducting this research to improve our abilities……..to compete against others."

"Others? You mean the Chinese or Russians?"

Manuela nearly choked on her reply. "No, he was talking about beings from other worlds."

"He actually said that?"

Dr. Faro seemed surprised. "No, he didn't have to say it; I assumed it in the context of our conversation," she explained. "Broderick went on to suggest that brain and soul integration unlocks our understanding of energy states in unprecedented ways. I guess at the point of integration, physics gets unified and you begin to learn how everything in the universe works. He inferred other beings are already there."

"Did you ever see this colonel again?"

"No."

"Did you ever see Varese again?"

"Yes, once in Miami and once again last year in Buenos Aires."

"Anything odd happen?"

"No, but the recruitment phase was clearly over," Manuela said, seemingly offended. "I was not wanted in their organization, not after the Thomas Broderick affair."

"When did you see Varese again?"

"In Miami, I ran into him at a forum on Nuclear Proliferation. We only said hello. In Argentina, he stayed as a guest of Vicente Rubie, as did I, at Corte Provence, the resort."

I knew of this man. "Vicente Rubie, the head of the Argentine National Academy of Sciences?" I asked. "He's a serious power broker and one of the world's leading experts on the UFO phenomenon."

"Very good, Mr. Jordan. Rubie is the most influential man in Argentina. We were lovers once and have shared many secrets."

"What did Varese say at Corte Provence?"

"Well, at the time I thought it bizarre. Remember, I've been to Patagonia and I've seen some unexplainable things; flying craft, saucer shaped discs, objects defying our logic with their speeds and maneuvers. Varese told me that if reports ever appeared in the media about UFO sightings at a time of worldwide tumult, to be a calming voice to my millions of admirers. Now is such a time, Mr. Jordan."

"I've read the Patagonia accounts as well. Patagonia is a hotbed of UFO activity and Rubie used to have an estate there."

Manuela recalled something from her mind. "The Americans came down to Patagonia to investigate," she said ruminating, "immediately after the last wave of sightings. Vicente still owns the estate; that's where the Americans stayed. Pictures were taken and Rubie sent some of the pictures to me as a favor. Thomas Broderick was in one of them, unidentified of course, dressed as a civilian."

I was stunned. "Was Varese in any of the pictures?"

"Yes, all of them."

"Do you think Varese knew this day was coming?"

Manuela's eyes brightened. "I do," she said excitedly, "his inner circle is connected at the highest levels. I don't even think Thomas Broderick is in the military, yet he has complete access to military cover and operations. They know astonishing amounts about the UFO phenomenon, more so than governments."

"Speculate for me."

Manuela rose abruptly. She stared at me without losing her enthusiasm. "No, Mr. Jordan, I have said enough," she said. "The rest you must do on your own. I have given you the background, but you must fill in the pieces."

"That's not enough to go on."

"Yes, it is. I have told you all I know, probably more than I should have. Stavenen, Gibson, Faro, and Straka are not in the circle, but you've been invited."

"Invited to what?"

"To the secret room," she declared, "the place where all our questions get answered. Inside that room is our collective future. This little global trek of yours is their way of making you earn it. But make no mistake about it; they want you badly. I'm envious, Mr. Jordan, I wish I was you."

Dr. Faro began to walk out of the room. She seemed emotionally distant, even hurt. "May I call on you if I need your services again?" I asked, probing her for confirmation. "You may still have a role to play."

"No, you may not call on me, but rest at my river retreat. You've been doing lots of flying, so relax here on the Iguaza to prepare yourself for Valhalla; my servants will attend to your every need. I leave in the morning for a conference in Lima. Mr. Freeman will be here early afternoon the day after tomorrow to transport you to Buenos Aires."

"Wait, Dr. Faro, is there anything wrong? You seem so removed."

Manuela went as sullen as Electra. "Please forgive me, Mr. Jordan, it's nothing personal, but not only did you reject my advances, you're a reminder," she responded glumly. "I've waited for years to gain passage to the secret room; in fact it's been a dream of mine. I figured their cabal might exist, and I've earned the right to sit at their table. But you're the one who gets to go. Good night, Mr. Jordan, and good luck."

ELEVEN

Associated Press—Moscow, Russia

September 12, 2017

The Russian government today admitted that an undisclosed amount of biological weaponry is missing from the old Soviet stockpile. Experts believe the amount could be sufficient to make ten to twelve biological weapons, each capable of devastating populations numbering in the tens of millions. The government here has categorically denied that sufficiency, indicating the true number is substantially less, on the order of three to five weapons. Moreover, Anton Mershev, the Russian deputy foreign minister and the leading expert on the old Soviet stockpile, assured the press today the likelihood of the weapons falling into terrorist hands is highly unlikely; when pressed on Carte Blanche, the arms cartel most likely to possess such weaponry, Mershev closed the press conference and walked away without further comment.

The next morning after a marvelous swim in the river and ample time for Nicholas to have initiated the oscillator scans, the BMS system activated. It didn't have much life left in it. Quite frankly I was surprised the system had lasted this long. Implantations were still an inexact science and an Illick body is an incredible biological machine capable of impressive homeostasis and bodily correction. Eric Waller's immune system had probably surrounded the implant and was attacking the organic exterior; once the exterior was penetrated, the implant would dissolve almost immediately and all relay would be lost.

This would be the final transmission.

Eric was someplace indoors, in a colorless room; Joseph Turner Abrille was with him. Both were pacing.

"The weapons are delivered, although the detonators seem to have failed," Abrille said, stopping and leaning against a table.

"We didn't pay for failure," Eric said.

"Relax, everything will be fine. The housing for the weapons disintegrates after activation, a precaution against detonator failure."

Eric roamed the room again. "So how long?" he asked, coming to a window and pausing. "When will these canisters finally blow?"

"I would say a few hours at most."

"Any chance the weapons have been defused?"

Abrille shrugged his shoulders. "I suppose, but your men reported precise placement," he said. "So I don't see how they could have been disarmed."

"So what now?"

Abrille slowly massaged his goatee. "We wait until people get sick," he responded. "That shouldn't be long now. You'll see."

At that moment, Anthony Rembacule stormed in. He slammed the door behind him. "The detonations have failed," he said angrily, castigating Abrille with his glance.

"We know," Eric responded, his words meant to calm the situation. "The housing is breaking down, the viruses released shortly. Abrille says just a few more hours."

"He's lying," Rembacule said, his voice rising, ignoring the tenor of his superior. "Breakdown should have occurred by now, people sickening or dying. There should have been reports by the media and yet there is nothing."

Both of the Illick turned to Abrille. "We have been over this," Abrille answered, trying to assuage both of them, "so please, let's all try and be patient."

Rembacule walked slowly toward Abrille, finally standing directly in front of him. He stared at him and his eyes turned metallic.

"What?" Abrille asked him, "I have told you what I know."

There was no response. Rembacule simply struck once to Abrille's neck and I heard the crack of bone and Abrille crumpled to the floor. The Illick have a devastating hand strike, three to four times the power of the most forceful human punch; Abrille was dead.

"I did not give that order," Eric shouted at Rembacule, "now he's no good to us."

"He never was."

Eric stepped over the body and came directly in front of Rembacule. "You are trying me," he yelled. "This is your last instance of *Basheske*."

Basheske is the Illick word for insubordination within the highest ranks. The arbiter has the authority to kill on the spot; Eric Waller was cleared for it, Rembacule was not.

With lightning speed, Eric thrust his hand at Rembacule's throat, holding it only inches from choking him. I thought he might strike. Surprised by the suddenness of the maneuver, Rembacule had no defense. Eric glared into Rembacule's eyes. Then, just as quickly, Eric Waller lowered his arm. "I will spare you this one final time," Eric said, decompressing. "But never test me again. Now, what do you think went wrong?"

Rembacule breathed in deeply, obviously relieved, searching for the proper words to answer.

"I think the Russians beat Carte Blanche again," he said.

"Explain."

"Well, we know the viruses were tested on the people Abrille kidnapped and used as guinea pigs. We saw that ourselves."

"Yes, the prostitutes and drug addicts, they all died."

"They did. But I think the entire stockpile degraded shortly thereafter. It probably lost its full potency weeks ago, perhaps longer."

Eric Waller waited a long interval before speaking. He looked distraught. "Did you send our team back to find the canisters?" he asked.

"I did."

"What did they find?"

"They can't locate them. The last search was just a few minutes ago."

Eric Waller walked around and once again came to face Anthony Rembacule. I have followed Eric for years, studying his moves and his expressions, and I had never seen him as resigned. "They won't locate the canisters," he said disappointedly. "The canisters were taken. The virus in them didn't degrade."

"Then what happened?" Rembacule asked, dismayed.

"The mission was compromised."

"By whom, who could have outsmarted us?"

Eric was a general viewing the battle below from a lofty hill, watching his army overrun and slaughtered, defeat inevitable. His face filled with regrettable comprehension. "David Jordan," he said dejectedly. "He had the humans scan their cities for biological weapons; that's how the canisters were found and disarmed. I am sure of it."

Rembacule stepped back, seemingly horrified. "We took every precaution," he said, debating the final result with the painstaking planning so characteristic of the Illick, "so it's impossible he knew our plans. We're better than him."

Eric rubbed his eyes, his mind scrolling through events, squinting as he recounted the possibilities, and then it came to him.

"No, David Jordan has a method, something in us, some technology perhaps, possibly an implant or a nanosensor," Eric said, conjuring thoughts. "He must have a device or heuristic methodology we didn't contemplate; it's the only way possible he could have known our plans. It's like he was with us."

"But how can that be?" Rembacule asked. "Our body security is the envy of the galaxy and our strategy simulations are unparalleled."

Eric Waller threw his head back. His impenetrable veneer seemed utterly punctured. "I don't know, but we blew our greatest opportunity," he said regretfully. "Now we will have to answer for our mistake."

"No, there must be some way—"

Eric waved a finger at Anthony Rembacule, stopping any other considerations. "There isn't another way, so reassemble our team. We are going home. We cannot be on Earth when David Jordan files his report. I won't be far behind you, not more than a few days. I have to get even with that bastard first and I think I know just how to do it."

TWELVE

Associated Press—Beijing, China

September 13, 2017

The Chinese government this morning rejected German Prime Minister Gerhard Wilboken's plea for a global summit in Munich, Germany, citing Germany's complicity in furthering Japan's nuclear capability and in providing India with Advanced Weapons Technology (AWT), including Electromagnetic Pulse and Microwave Disintegration battlefield systems. Germany, India, and Japan denied any such linkage although the Chinese have offered to provide proof within days.

Separately, independent news agencies reported a wave of UFO sightings over the Chinese capital late last evening. The government here denied that anything "unfamiliar" occurred in the nighttime sky, although residents here were reportedly terrified and took to the streets in protest. Chinese riot police were sent in around midnight to quell a "labor strike" although all of the major unions and workers associations denied any such activity. At 9:00 a.m. this morning, the government here declared a state of martial law and will implement a curfew for the evening hours.

Manuela was certainly prescient about relaxing on the wondrous banks of the Iguaza River; never in my life have I felt such respite and rejuvenation. It also didn't bother me that Eric Waller wanted to even the score; that was just a continuation of the status quo, where he had wanted to kill me for years. So I guess you could say I was unruffled. I figured Eric would lay a trap on Aueretern, a vacation planet I was to visit shortly, where the treaty between The Council and the Illick was unenforceable. He couldn't kill me on Earth because the treaty stipulated that condition, but on Aueretern there were no rules. He was probably going to remain behind on Earth for a few days to confirm my travel plans and then depart for Illician. Shortly thereafter, he would arrive in Aueretern. I uploaded a report regarding my suspicions of his plans for me at Aueretern and immediately Ambassador Wren rescheduled my vacation and sent a security team to Aueretern with hopes to place another implant into Eric's brain.

Knowing Dr. Faro and I had correctly surmised the right cities as targets added to my repose that morning, although the Illick were like viruses themselves, fully capable of regenerating and regaining their potency at any given moment in time. Someday, I knew I would have to fight them again. And there was still Nicholas and a world on the verge of nuclear annihilation and the possibility of lost human innocence, so just as quickly as it had begun my dawdling ended as duty called.

Just after the noon hour, I gathered my belongings and waited for my ride to Buenos Aires. Soon, I heard the rotor blades of a helicopter and saw Mr. Freeman emerge.

"Good afternoon," he yelled over to me. "Enjoy your stay?"

"Yes, very much," I responded, "I wish it had been longer."

"No time for that, you have to be in Miami."

"Not you too," I said, placing my things in the helicopter.

Mr. Freeman assisted me. "I made your plane reservations and your flight leaves in a few hours, so we must hurry," he said. "You don't have to thank me."

"Then I won't, just get me there safely. You did it once; tell me you can do it again."

This time, Mr. Freeman flew high above the river and we did little sightseeing. We spoke only a few sentences as I read a brief Manuela had prepared for me regarding Franco Varese and her experience with secret societies. My hope for human innocence was now down to one man. In exactly two hours, I boarded my plane at Ezeiza and flew for half a day over the Atlantic Ocean and well into Floridian airspace before the final descent into Miami International.

Although the flight was uneventful and smooth, in that descent I felt emptiness in my soul that had to be death.

The image came to me again, of clawing at the ground in the hills near my mountain home, the world becoming a senseless blur all around me, as I questioned my life and the absurdity of living. Some type of answer filled the trees. I lay on my hands and knees and wallowed in the dirt, crying helplessly as my soul drowned in horrific sorrow. I felt nauseous. I felt emptiness. The feeling of personal insignificance was like a desert sandstorm darkening the light and I wondered how I might survive without the presence of the sun. I remembered bleeding and choking as I lay gasping in the forest loam, unable to move. I barely recall disembarking from the aircraft or finding my way through the airport as the visions of terror filled my mind.

"Are you okay?" a passerby at baggage claim asked me.

"Yes, just a little hazy from my flight."

"I know the feeling," the man said commiserating. "My pilot had to be drunk. Guy was an arrogant ass, too."

I think I laughed. "Thanks for your concern," I said to him appreciatively.

The man left with a look of compassion, joining what appeared to be a group of coworkers for a conference or convention.

I sat down in an airport guest chair. For a moment, I wondered if I was going crazy. In rare cases, members of my kind have experienced "adaptive malfunction," as the atmosphere here can occasionally cause our brains to erode due to protracted exposure to trace elements of argon and neon. Tests had shown I had a mild susceptibility. If so, I would have to leave Earth and of course leave Jenny behind as well. I wouldn't be able to return for many years as my brain recuperated. If forced to leave, I resolved to tell Jenny the truth: about my past, what I was, the story of The Council, my mission here, everything about me that she had never known. That would violate my primary directive, but I wasn't leaving her without telling her the full story, even if it meant her choosing another path without me. Jenny deserved that much.

Of course, I could be having presentiments, but presentiments of what? In the past all my divinations were at worst neutral glimpses of the future, but these were horrific and unprecedented.

So I tried not to think about it.

Finally after twenty minutes the feeling subsided.

Waiting for my luggage on the carousel and still a bit shaky, I received an urgent text message from Nicholas. How he knew I was in Miami I do not know. But the message was direct, even for him.

In Miami myself. Meet me at Damon's at 8. Be there. No excuses.

I figured Nicholas had the Deputy Secretary, Kashee Haldyiha, an Ethiopian and a well-respected negotiator, conduct in his absence the now televised emergency session at the United Nations and the subsequent press conference held before the world's media. For Nicholas to miss that much spotlight spelled trouble of the biggest kind.

Damon's is one of those swanky restaurants you find in every metropolitan downtown; stuffy, horribly overpriced, with embarrassingly small portions, and the lighting is always absurdly straining, making me increasingly moody as I walked back to find Nicholas surrounded by three large bodyguards and some kind of secret service agent. Nicholas rose to greet me.

"For once you're on time," he said.

"Nice seeing you too."

We sat down at the table. Nicholas waved off his bodyguards and the secret service agent. "Please excuse my gang here," he said to me, "but the U.N. security detail was beefed up because of threats on my person. Who'd want to kill me?"

"How much time do you have?"

"Don't tease me now," Nicholas said, so faintly I could barely hear him. "I'm much too fragile these days."

"Sorry."

Nicholas regrouped himself. "Well, the good news is that the scans worked; we found the canisters of biological weapons and defused them," he said, summoning some cheer. "How the hell you pulled that off, I have no idea."

I actually felt sorry for him. Nicholas' eyes drooped like a basset hound in August swelter.

"Then why aren't you ecstatic?" I asked him. "We found the canisters."

"One crisis averted, replaced by another."

"We just saved hundreds of millions of lives."

Nicholas shook his head. "My experts said the viruses were sub standard," he said. "Still millions may have been killed, so I do thank you."

I felt like jumping down this throat, but he looked so low I decided to forget it. "Well, I've made some progress in solving your global crisis," I reported. "Manuela Faro was particularly helpful. She gave me a name that—"

"That will have to wait. Do you know Vladimir Arezsky?"

"Sure, the Russian oil minister. Former KGB second, member of the Politburo, and a lifetime pal of Putin. I met him once in Sevastopol. He's a wealthy man."

Nicholas leaned in. "This stays confidential, but Arezsky is their Armand Hammer, with friends in high places," he said. "He has a mole in the Chinese military. He wouldn't tell me his name. Anyway, this mole told Arezsky the Chinese have determined this conflict is going nuclear and have developed a first strike plan to cripple India and then Japan. Diplomatically, they deduce they can neutralize Moscow with financial concessions; if not, the contingency plan calls for nuclear strikes on Asiatic Russia to keep the Russians in Europe."

"So the Chinese are using the current crisis as a pretext for Asian hegemony?"

"That's how it looks."

Nicholas and I just looked at each other, the gravity of the scenario hitting us. "What do you make of Nakashima's visit to Washington to see President Rice?" I eventually asked.

"Strategizing what to do if the Chinese launch a first strike against Japan. We're at that point."

That seemed logical. In the last week, it had seemed that China was going for broke; her aggressive actions were unprecedented and audacious. "I heard the Australian navy sank three Chinese cargo ships and two patrol boats in the South China Sea," I said.

"Yes," Nicholas answered. "And the Americans have given the Australians nuclear weapons."

"Are you sure?"

"Positive. The Australians might use them to protect their investments in South Korea by launching against North Korea."

"Have Chinese and American forces fired on each other in the Taiwan Strait? I thought I heard that as well."

Nicholas clasped his hands together, fretting. "My intelligence people tell me there are nuclear submarines colliding with each other," he said gloomily. "We could be days, even hours, from a thermonuclear exchange."

All I could think of was innocence lost. Humans were dangerously close.

I took a chance. "Nicholas, what do you make of the UFO sightings?" I asked him.

Nicholas turned a shade paler. "Why that has to come now, I don't know. We have study groups on the phenomenon at the U.N."

"What's your guess as to their intent?"

Nicholas made sure his guards were out of earshot. "Theories say that in global crises UFOs make themselves known as a diversion to war, but these are only theories," he stated. "I can't even imagine throwing the extraterrestrial issue into this quagmire."

I let it go. "So what do you need me to do?"

Nicholas had turned especially dour as he told me of Arezsky and the Chinese threat. He grabbed at his stomach in discomfort.

"This crisis is killing me, David," he said. "I have a bleeding ulcer and my nerves are shot. The world is blowing up on my watch and I am powerless to stop it."

"What about your advisory group?"

"Every scenario we run through ends in nuclear annihilation. So what do I need you to do? I need you to fucking solve it for me."

I felt frustrated. I had been led through hoops, but for what result? "I am trying, you know, but this is one hell of a mess," I said. "Every day, it escalates further; it's like there's no stopping the negative spiral."

Nicholas dipped his napkin into his glass of water and wiped his face. He sat up on his haunches, as desperate as he was exasperated.

"David, ever since Williams I knew there was something special about you," he said beseechingly. "You had no family. Oh, I know you spoke of far distant relatives, which I never met by the way, but I always knew you were alone in this world. I had plenty of backing, but you were always better with people, deeper in comprehension, more transcendent, everything. Everyone spoke of how gifted you were. I know—."

"Stop, you don't have to bullshit me, Nicholas."

He ignored me. "I don't have much sincerity left in me, but I swear you've always been my idol," he said. "Some connection you make will bring the solution to our problems. It's not just for me; it's for an entire planet. I'm begging you."

It's been hard being alone. Nicholas saw my loneliness all these many years. He knew me like few others. I never had a family, not a real one anyway, and I sure as hell can't count Donald Niebauer or Ambassador Wren as any family of mine. The Council dropped me here as a young man because I had premonitions of Nicholas and some future importance of his life. That's why I was at Williams College. That's why I met him in the first place. Now, all these years later, I still don't know if my premonitions will lead to human self-determination or our intervention to save this planet from itself. I just know it's a critical time.

"David?" Nicholas pleaded with me. "Are you still here?"

I wouldn't have regrets of families lost or families that never were had it not been for Jenny and the love she showed her mother during her battle with cancer. I remember feeling robbed of never having felt the way Jenny felt or having someone to thank for the days of my living. Because of Jenny, somewhere inside I stung.

I rose from the table. "One more interview, Nicholas, and then I'll solve your crisis," I said. "Just another day or two, I promise."

"Does this interview lead to Miami? Is that why you're here?"

"I think so."

Nicholas breathed a sigh of relief. Color returned to his face. He rose and held out his hand.

"Don't let me down," he said. "Global business is grinding to a halt. Half the world is rioting or dying on battlefields. Next, we get mushroom clouds and vaporization. We're almost finished as a species."

Nicholas trusted me and I found it particularly ironic that a man few on Earth have trusted would place the fate of an entire planet in his lifelong trust of me. There is more irony there than I can possibly explain.

"Nicholas, I must go."

"But wait, what is your plan? How can I be sure it will work?"

"Goodbye Nicholas."

When I walked out of Damon's and into the balmy Miami evening, I thought of Manuela Faro and another of the universe's many ironies: I trusted her and in the name she had given to me. In the low, droopy clouds hanging over the city I actually saw the man's name reflected high in the nighttime sky.

For innocence now belonged to one Franco Varese and in my entreaty to The One I prayed he was everything Manuela thought him to be.

*   *   *

To my amazement I had a message on my cell phone from the man in question; Franco Varese wanted to meet me the following evening at his institute and I was to come alone and come prepared. Prepared for what I hadn't a clue. Manuela had arranged the meeting; Varese claimed to be looking forward to our discussion as one anticipates 'a walk with an old friend.' There was no urgency in his voice, but he mentioned he had only been days away from contacting me on his own. I found that most peculiar.

I also had a message from Donald Niebauer. As usual, his tone was grating and filled with its usual desperation and whininess. Although a voice mail, it sounded like an old teletype:

"It's Donald. You're failing. Intervention is imminent. I have advised Ambassador Wren to activate CX. Uploads are late and ambiguous. Advise of your status."

I should have been furious. Yet deep inside of me my usual skepticism gave way to the slightest ray of hope innocence might somehow be spared. I wondered if perhaps humans had one final card to play. I looked into the stars before entering my hotel and a wonderful thought crossed my mind: *maybe, just maybe, Miami was the biggest surprise of all.*

*   *   *

I kicked around until late afternoon and then drove the half hour to *The Institute for Human Advancement* that Franco Varese oversaw as its director. The ride down was joyous. Turquoise inlets wove into cottony beaches and there is some kind of water tree with pretty burgundy leaves that tiptoes into the sea around every bend. Terns flew everywhere. Some seemed to be following me. Finally I came to the prettiest cove of the day; her name was etched on a sign, surrounded by sea flowers, *Serenity*.

The Institute was a simple three story glass building overlooking a small tarn of foamy beige sea water. Other businesses occupied the building; software startups, financial service companies, defense contractors, and one environmental services firm named Enviroland that I knew well. They were heavily involved with the CIA on a contract basis and conducted resource extraction for a variety of oil and energy companies.

I took the elevator up to the third floor. Around the far corner was the Office of the Director. I walked through the door of the office and heard a chime. A door ahead of me and slightly to the right opened, and a short man with a bald head and a handsomely tanned face emerged. His eyes were soft and he glimpsed me quickly.

"David Jordan," the man said, "Manuela said you have amazing presence and she was correct."

"You must be Franco Varese. I'm pleased to meet you, sir."

He did not shake my hand, but rather patted my arm. "And I am very pleased to meet you," he said, easing away. "Please, step into my office and we can chat."

The office looked out onto the olive lagoon. We sat on opposite chairs across from his desk. On the desk were bottles of water and two glasses, the water poured, with ice in the glasses. His fingernails were immaculately groomed and his hands strong and vascular. Although I was a bit nervous, he seemed as calm as a lull in a storm.

"Mr. Jordan, understand I am fully apprised of your mission," he started. "I have known of you for years."

"You have?"

"Yes, I was a fan of your proposed think tank and your selection of Stavenen, Gibson, and Faro as its faculty emeritus."

"That was some time ago."

"Yes, it was. You're a particularly talented man."

"Thank you."

Franco Varese grinned. "Then here is your reward," he remarked, his eyes twinkling in the low light. "You will learn the real purpose of my institute and be made aware of our 'master plan.' You will hear things here tonight never suspected. Are you ready to begin?"

I marveled at how such a soft voice contained so much power. He possessed astonishing grace and seemed incredibly comfortable. "Sure," I finally answered, warming to him.

"Good. Let me start by saying that on appearances the Institute is designed to advance human knowledge and understanding. In reality, we control human events."

A freight train hit me. It wasn't just his incredibly bold and even absurd statement, but rather an overwhelming sense he was telling the truth. The room shifted on its own.

"That's right, Mr. Jordan, I am the leader of an organization connected at the highest levels in every major country on Earth," he said. "We have a network of business tycoons, intelligence chiefs, military leaders, journalists, publishers, government officials, financiers, you name it Mr. Jordan, and we have them. Not everyone, mind you, only the ones we deem significant and worthy of our organization. We are that higher cabal everyone suspects exists, but no one can prove. Christopher Thrattas is our man in Greece. I had him call you once to steer you to Stavenen and she of course led you to Gibson. Then of course it was Faro next and then to me. We sent our little notes and correspondences and the rest is history."

I remembered the call I took on a balcony out with Jenny at her favorite restaurant in San Francisco. I had talked to Thrattas then.

"I feel used," I said in jest, still gauging his credibility.

Franco Varese straightened a wrinkle in his pants, nonchalantly. "We all get used. You were tested, by your time with Stavenen, Gibson, and Faro."

"Tested? For what purpose?"

"Well, this predicament before us is very significant," Franco Varese commented. "So we wanted to hear what each of these brilliant minds had to say on the subject of building human harmony during times of intense crisis. All three are some of the world's best experts on international relations, but from differing perspectives of course. We welcome diverse opinion. Your interviews were the best format we could devise and their assessments will help us in the future. But more importantly, we wanted to test your moxie."

"Were their offices wired?"

"Yes, fully bugged, even the river retreat. You see, Mr. Socorro is also one of ours."

"Well, I'll be damned," I said, recalling my time with Mr. Socorro. "He was kind of a sneaky bastard. I liked him though. Say, why not get Stavenen, Gibson, and Faro to join you here?"

Franco Varese shook his head. "No, Stavenen is too infatuated with the U.N., Gibson much too set in his ways, and we tried to lure Dr. Faro a few years ago but she has too much light on her. But all have much to say and feeding off each other through sequential interviewing in the specific order we deemed was marvelously informative. Plus, we got to know you instead of presuming your character."

"Well, I hope I contributed to a deeper understanding of human nature," I said, pleased with my past performance.

"Oh, you did, Mr. Jordan, and your interaction with Stavenen we found particularly intriguing; she believed you were a being from the stars and you used your meditative powers to 'heal' her. If she lives longer than her prognosis, we may put you in charge of our human health division," Franco Varese concluded with a crafty grin.

I had to cover fast. "How do you know about my experiences with Eastern medicine and my fascination with transpersonal psychology?" I asked him. "I kept my interest in those subjects secret from everyone."

Franco Varese simply grinned again. "Oh, Mr. Jordan, we know of your time in Tibet and all about your curious eyes."

"What about my eyes?"

Franco Varese rubbed the back of his neck, seemingly bored. "Your genetic anomaly, the golden flecks in your eyes," he said. "They are quite unique, perhaps the only such eyes on Earth."

"Do my eyes scare you?"

Once again, a little grin. "Hardly," he commented, as cavalier as a poker player with a winning hand. "I have a cousin with perfect triangles on his forearms and a sister with a group of moles that form the letter G, so nature plays its little tricks."

Satisfied, my identity was still a secret, I had to revisit the interviews. "Back up a minute, you actually bugged their offices?" I asked him.

"Yes, Mr. Jordan, we heard everything. Why is that so hard to believe? Wiring an office is as easy as a visit to a dentist. You passed with flying colors."

"Then you knew about the Carte Blanche plot?"

"No, that is why you are here," Varese responded, perking up. "That showed us your capabilities; quite impressive, I might add."

"So you're organization is vulnerable to terrorism?"

Franco Varese sighed. "Yes and no," he replied. "Terrorism can still damage the world, take for instance 9/11 and the recent soccer stadium attack in Paris, but we weakened biological weapons potency years ago with a 'trade secret' of ours. Those molecules are now a constant part of our atmosphere. Still, you saved tens of thousands of lives, so job well done, Mr. Jordan."

"So how do you coordinate world events?" I asked him, remembering his bold statement from earlier in our conversation.

Franco Varese brought us the two waters with ice. He gave one to me. "We circumvent governments when we must, but we generally work through existing channels."

"Ever had to kill anyone?" I asked.

The man in front of me smiled a devious smile. "Mr. Jordan, we do whatever we have to do to meet our objectives."

"What was the impetus to form such an organization?"

"Two things Mr. Jordan," Franco Varese said quickly, sitting back down, relaxing again. "So listen and listen carefully: nuclear weapons and the UFO phenomenon."

I sat up straighter. "That seems simple enough," I concluded.

For the first time, the man paused. His eyes beheld mine like gravity. "Well actually, it was assessment made by my predecessors back in the 1940s," he said. "Human behavior was flawed and our codes of law and social values were inadequate to meet the challenges of living in a nuclear age."

I actually felt a few tingles. "That man's dark side had to be controlled in a nuclear world," I interjected.

"Yes, Mr. Jordan, Hitler proved that to us. So we needed an organization superseding nations, cultures, languages and religions and bonding the best of our 'better natures' into all of human civilization. Where the United Nations fails, we succeed."

"The respect for nuclear weapons I fully understand, but how does the UFO phenomenon come into play?"

"We have been watched for a very long time, Mr. Jordan. They watch us now."

"Watched by whom?" I asked. I was still astounded he trusted me enough to tell me this amazing story.

Again, there was no hesitation. "Of that, we are not entirely sure," he said. "We do know we have been visited by over twenty different species as of 2008. Humans have had direct interface with four types of beings since the 1950s. We're not sure which species is in charge."

Anybody else conversing with this man would have been on the floor. All I felt was hope surging through my body. I wanted to pinch myself.

"Which species do you think is in charge?" I asked him.

"Well, we know the grays, short with large wraparound black eyes, large heads and spindly long arms, are the most numerous. But we think the beings in charge may actually be rather human in appearance. We have our theories."

I saw Franco Varese felt like he was letting me in on a very large secret. His eyes glistened with excitement.

"Nothing can compare to what we humans are on the verge of discovering," he said, continuing on, without offering me a chance to interpolate. "Imagine, if you will, Mr. Jordan, the complexities of human relations magnified one hundred times in a galactic scheme beyond our wildest imaginations. Think of how interesting it all must be."

Once again, I had to ensure I wasn't discovered. "Can we go back one second to which extraterrestrial species is in charge?" I asked. "You mentioned one species is nearly human?"

"Oh yes, how rude of me. Indications are that a nearly human species supervises the other beings and has been assigned the primary management task in human observation because of their close similarities to our genotype. We suspect some may be living among us."

"No? Living on Earth?"

"Yes, we believe they'll intervene in our affairs if they perceive we are destroying the planet."

"Say as in a biological or nuclear war?"

I saw a raised eyebrow. "Yes, most specifically with nuclear weapons, as we don't think environmental degradation or natural calamity would cause their intervention. Their ongoing surveillance of Earth intensifies when human relations deteriorate to the point of possible nuclear devastation. Otherwise, it appears their policy is as nonjudgmental observer."

"Has a determination been made as to their possible hostility when human relations devolve to a possible nuclear conflagration?"

Franco Varese took a deep breath. For the first time, he looked outside. "Yes, we believe they are non-hostile, as it appears they don't covet our planet because of our natural resource base or some other survivability problem," he said. "No, from everything we can determine they adhere to a galactic code forbidding invasion or aggression. We suspect they might intervene if they had to, but the intervention would probably be so powerful as to render our weaponry useless."

I sat back in my chair. "Fascinating," I said, "how much of this is conjecture on your part?"

Mine was a pointed question, but Franco Varese never rattled or grew distant. "Again, we've had relations with a number of species for over fifty years," he said. "They haven't told us much, but there are occasional hints. We have some hardware of theirs, some translated texts, artifacts from their planet, and even a written history of the galaxy from their perspective. Our analysts have made our own *inferences*."

"These nearly human ones, have you seen one in the flesh?" I asked, measuring him.

The man in front of me shook his head ever so slowly. "No, but it has been a dream of mine. I've met the others, the advanced dinosaurs."

"You mean the grays?"

"Yes."

"So the dinosaur line of evolution is preeminent on most planets?"

"We believe so, yes."

"But not here, not after that asteroid collided with Earth sixty five million years ago and wiped out the dinosaurs. Otherwise, dinosaurs would have kept evolving here and become grays?"

"That is correct, as far as we know. Our evolutionary biologists believe that's the case. And why are you smiling?"

I caught myself a bit. "Well, I doubt grays would want to be called 'advanced dinosaurs,' that's all."

"That humans are more than monkeys?"

"Yes, something along those lines."

There was an awkward silence. We both stared at each other for a moment. "Fair enough," Franco Varese finally conceded, "but we should discuss the biggest monkey of all. That would be your good friend, Nicholas Straka."

* * *

Outside, the sun sat on the water and the world went magenta. It was the prettiest sunset I had seen in many years, a sunset of transformation as well as a sunset of anticipation, and one much more like a dawn than an ending to a day. If this man was telling me the truth, humans had a chance.

Not sure of what to say next and nervous about the UFO discussion, I glanced around the room. Pictures of his institute and its members hung on the walls.

"This is some little guild you have here," I said.

"Exactly Mr. Jordan, that's why you'll be joining us. We're going to make a hero out of your friend Straka, as much as it galls us to do so, since it's time for the United Nations to have a major success story for the world to share. His achievement will also provide us continued cover for our little organization, albeit unwittingly."

"Okay, so what's the plan for Nicholas?"

"Oh, it's really quite simple. We are giving you a list of names of key personnel in various countries along with a codeword you will pass along to Mr. Straka. He will then contact the names on the list, relaying the code-word, and the fun begins."

"What kind of fun is that?"

"Well, the key personnel contact members of the national security apparatus in each country and that country's leadership stands down at their direction. It's rather enjoyable watching them change their plans."

"What if they don't stand down?"

"There's a coup."

"The leadership agrees to this?"

Franco Varese took a drink of water. "Yes, all are told when they assume power they may have to someday follow the direction of a higher cabal," he said. "It's a condition of their power."

"Do they know the reason why?"

"No. And we don't bother in every country, Mr. Jordan. Only in the major countries do we actually control their governments with our network. Smaller nations are controlled through more traditional measures like geopolitics."

"Have you encountered any resistors within the cabal?"

"You mean a rogue?"

"Yes."

Franco Varese groaned. It was the first chink in his armor. "We have theorized it's possible," he said, "but remember our cabal is often a combination of actual heads of state and well as key individuals within the national security apparatus. It's a check and balance system. Could there be a miscalculation or some subversion that catches us unawares? Why yes, I suppose, but we're the highest evolved organization of our kind in human history, so I like our chances."

"Have you thought about whether another race of beings might subvert or otherwise influence a member of your cabal, especially one with his hands on the nuclear trigger? If you are certain there are other intelligent beings visiting Earth, might they have their own plans?"

Franco Varese cogitated for a moment, a worried look appeared on his face, and then strangely a solace came to his eyes. Much thought had occurred in his mind. "As I stated earlier, we believe the beings act as nonjudgmental observers," he said, "and we have no indications they have separate agendas from each other."

"What if you're wrong?"

The best of brilliant men keep their cool under fire, even when their concepts get waylaid. The man in front of me was an exceptional man, and where others might have been angered or frustrated, instead he sought understanding.

"Do you have something to tell me, Mr. Jordan? Something that relates either to beings or their intentions? That would interest me very much indeed."

It was time for some hierarchical reshuffling. "Yes, I do have something to tell you, but I need you to respond with truthfulness and trust me," I answered unhesitatingly. "You brought me here, so here me out."

Franco Varese leaned back in his chair and stared at me curiously. He surveyed me and made an internal decision. I saw it in his face. "The floor is yours," he finally said, acquiescently but graciously, "so please, speak your mind and speak the truth."

"Is Ghoshanad of Pakistan a member of your cabal?"

"Yes. Who told you?"

"He might not be anymore. The same applies for the second man you selected to monitor Ghoshanad."

Franco Varese scrutinized me with an intensity he hadn't shown. For the first time, he seemed adversarial. "You better be right, Mr. Jordan," he said, pointing his finger at me. "I don't take kindly to accusations against members of my little organization. Ghoshanad is an outward radical, but secretly he is one of our people. So is the other man. I hand selected them."

"Just check it out. My sources tell me both might be double agents and launch nuclear attacks against India if things worsen for Pakistan."

"Who are your sources, Mr. Jordan?"

"Trade secret, Mr. Varese. You have yours and I have mine. You're not the only one connected deeply in Pakistan. And my sources tell me Ghoshanad and the other man have been 'visited' by strange lights and meddling beings from far away. I know that sounds crazy, but I trust these sources with my life. Removing Ghoshanad from power is your safest bet."

Franco Varese gave a look of acknowledgment. I sensed from our verbal sparring he suddenly trusted me. "Fair enough," he said, "I will have my people look into it. If you are correct, we will take remedial action. I will tell you in a bit why your position is worth investigating. It has to do with your abilities. Do you have any other news?"

I smiled at him. "No, but I'm glad we understand each other," I said. "You may be wondering why I am not shocked by your revelations of extra-terrestrial beings?"

"The thought had crossed my mind."

I took a sip of water. "Well, your organization is not the only one studying the UFO phenomenon," I said. "Are you familiar with the SkySociety?"

Franco Varese straightened. "Yes, the UFO organization that tracks sightings and close encounters, with scientific field teams and an anonymous advisory board," he said. "Don't tell me you're a member."

"Oh, more than a member, Mr. Varese, I'm their chief consultant and also their largest guarantor. SkySociety has an incredibly vast database and performs meticulous research. They are their own cabal; not as high as this one it seems, but they have transcended the authorities and broken the law many times and don't seem to care. Ghoshanad and the other man are in their case studies. Between you and me, SkySociety has hardware and has conducted autopsies on a variety of beings. They know just slightly less than the U.S. Air Force."

"Well, I'll be damned. We've thought about penetrating them, but the Air Force usually sends us what we need. Although, with this information, we may rethink that. Is there anything else, Mr. Jordan?"

The case studies factoid was a lie; I had the information on Ghoshanad from Donald Niebauer and The Council, so it was time to change the subject. "No, nothing else on that subject," I responded. "So let's see now, where were we?"

"We were talking about the plan for Nicholas and leaders standing down where necessary."

"Oh yes, tell me more about that."

* * *

Franco Varese logged into his computer, calling up a file. I saw a picture of Nicholas when he opened it. "Well, the United Nations will restore borders, territories, sovereignty in the case of Taiwan and the Himalayan countries, and will compel all sides to negotiate in good faith," he explained. "Like I said, it's all really quite simple."

I had seen this same dynamic in other worlds. Species lasting through time sublimate their individual interests to the collective good, usually through a supra organization or some other world group. But this was the first time I had encountered a clandestine organization fulfilling that function.

"That's fair enough, but still, why me?" I asked him. "Why am I involved in all this?"

Franco Varese gave me a sly peek, turning the monitor on his computer toward my direction. He pointed to the picture of Nicholas. "You were our best course of action," he said, gently patting his hands in front of his mouth. "Your connection to Straka is critical for our purposes. Our goal is to gradually pull humanity into an understanding of the extraterrestrial presence so that we can be welcomed into the galactic brotherhood."

"I'm confused. How does that goal affect Straka and me?"

Franco Varese returned to his seat, leaning back. "This time the public will see the United Nations as successfully solving both the current global crisis and the recent spate of UFO activity, which will subside when this conflict is resolved," he said. "The first realization will be overt and the second more subtle. Always gradual, Mr. Jordan, but eventually humanity will make the necessary linkages and know we're not alone in the universe."

"That will be a hard reality for humans to accept."

"Not if given enough time."

I scratched my forehead. "Nicholas has others around him, even a few friends and close supporters," I added, knowing Nicholas limited his circle on purpose. "I mean, there are a few. Why was I the best course of action? I'm fairly well known and that could bring attention."

Franco Varese laughed aloud. "Because Straka trusts you," he said, seemingly giddy in the notion that most people in government despised Nicholas. "You have more influence over him than anyone else we know. And that influence is rare. He is, after all, perhaps the world's biggest jackass, and he trusts almost no one."

The man in front of me calmly waited for my response. "Something tells me you have something else important to say," I said.

Franco Varese cracked his knuckles, relaxed his hands, and then cracked them again. "I do have something to say. It's time to tell you what your role will be here in our little organization. We've wanted you to join us for a long time."

*   *   *

Nighttime had fallen. The magenta glow had turned to purplish ember and higher in the sky the night had deepened into starry blackness. Like so many innumerable stars, another day had passed into yet another infinite night. The nights of time are like grains of sand on an endless shore, so many as to be incalculable to all but The One, and it's left for us who must one day pass from this life to recognize those most wonderful of moments so granted to us.

"This has been some discussion," Franco Varese said to me, directly on cue. "You now understand why you were selected and here is your role."

"You want me to replace you someday?" I joked again, imagining the irony of my being in charge of the world. The Council of course would forbid it.

Franco Varese gave his nose a tug, engaging in my banter with his gaze. "Perhaps in time you can retire me, but more importantly we have analyzed your writings in trade journals and scholarly publications and we are astounded at your abilities," he said.

"Come now, they're just articles," I threw in, wondering where this was going.

This time his ear got a tug. "No truly, Mr. Jordan, no reason for humility," he said encouragingly. "Where you have invested, what you have advised, most of it is absolutely brilliant stuff, and we concluded no one on Earth makes your associations. You're phenomenal, uncannily prescient."

"Thank you, it has always come naturally."

The man looked past me when he spoke his next words. "In fact, your observations and advocacies are rather anonymous and we like that as well. Personal fame is counter to our purposes. You're known, but not that well known. But if your work were more widely dispersed, and hence known, it would act as an accelerator for our desensitization plan."

"And you want to put your foot on me, give your desensitization plan more gas?"

Franco Varese resisted, but still amiably. "No Mr. Jordan, we do everything incrementally," he said. "Slightly more acceleration, yes, but not more than humanity can handle at any given moment. Our time horizon is quite long. No, we want to learn your abilities and template them so our leadership makes quantum leaps in their analytical capabilities."

"Why is that?"

The man in front of me sipped his water while his stare wandered into the ether world. "Well, because through enhanced associative abilities we might learn *their* intentions and purposes here," he said.

"You mean the UFOs?"

Franco Varese walked over to the window and glanced upward into the nighttime sky. "Yes," he said longingly. He turned back to face me and spoke again. "Not long ago, you wrote a piece regarding the role of observation in capital allocation, measuring returns versus pro forma expectations, with new mathematical formulas, across various industries in diverse parts of the world. Do you remember that study?"

"Sure, the goal was to better reallocate capital through enhanced observational techniques."

Franco Varese breathed a pleasurable breath. "Yes, you established a strong correlation between more thorough observation and increased financial returns," he said. "In a more general sense, you accelerated 'observational studies,' a discipline with growing influence."

"Thank you for noticing. The premise is that observing is causal to greater returns, whereas prior thinking posited observing as neutral."

"Yes, we learned that observation is never neutral."

"So you agree with my premise?"

Franco Varese seemed as a man recently acquiring a fortune. "Well, sit back and listen to our discovery," he said, "you will find it quite amazing."

I did as instructed, relaxing a bit. I hadn't taken any notes and because this wasn't a formal interview, I didn't have my recorder. The conversation had been so engaging I hadn't cared.

"Mr. Jordan, not only is observation never neutral, but it is *designed*. We asked ourselves 'what if the UFOs are observing us and trying for a higher return over time through their observations? Does their increased observation in crises lead to some kind of higher return?' Using your formulas, we determined their observations of the Artic icepacks led to our expanding awareness of global warming. Their swarming over key nuclear missile sites in North Korea and Pakistan allowed us to discover these locations and bring them to the world's attention through the United Nations. Massive UFO activity in Kota Bharu, Malaysia alerted us to a terrorist bioweaponry lab with vast destructive potential."

"Observations were clustered?"

"Yes, what we learned is their observations are concentrated to send us messages; the higher return they seek is either our survival or the Earth's sustainability. And we would have never conducted the study without your work. Your formulas and concepts were pure genius."

"What does the job pay?"

This time, Franco Varese exploded into a radiant pink laugh. He took some time to regain himself. "A billion 'thanks' and your expenses fully paid," he said. "It will be great having such a successful businessman work with us."

"That reminds me; how are you funded?"

Suddenly, I received a blank stare. "Like any intelligence organization, Mr. Jordan, we are highly compartmentalized," he said. "The answer to your last question is above your security clearance. Do you have any other questions?"

I took a chance. "Have you thought I might be an extraterrestrial?"

This time I saw an obfuscated look and some type of remembrance. "Well, your lack of medical records is very curious," he said. "But you pay your taxes on time and your golf swing has a wicked slice. Your girlfriend is a beautiful young woman from San Francisco and you have a dreadful fear of flying. Oh, I almost forgot, you drink cocktails on occasion. That's human enough for us."

"Go on, this is getting interesting. You've been spying on me."

Franco Varese went suddenly stern and his eyes signaled disapproval. "The biggest mystery is your relationship with Straka," he said. "You feel indebted to this man, a man you consider corrupt and unprincipled, when you yourself are so ethical and honorable. That fact we struggled with more than any other variable."

I cleared my throat. "Nicholas has his value, and half on the world seems to agree with me," I said. "And although he's incorrigible, he's in your plans as well. So if what you say is true, we are wasting time."

Franco Varese rubbed his balding head. "Oh, it's true enough," he said forthrightly. "And you are right, Mr. Jordan, it's time to set our plan into motion."

* * *

Franco Varese, for what I had observed in the short time I knew him, was a man supremely assured of his importance without any ego. He was smoothly methodical. Not one to dally, he briskly made his way over to his desk and took an envelope from the top desk drawer. He reached across and handed me the envelope.

"Open it," he said.

I did as instructed. Inside the envelope was a simple sheet of white paper with the names of men and women on a far left column and their home country listed on the right edge of the paper. In the middle column was a phone number for each contact. At the bottom, was a word bolded in red, PROCEED. The list was printed from a word document on a computer, but the word in red was stamped bright and bold.

"Remember, give the contact list to Straka as well as the codeword and tell him to contact each name on your sheet of paper using the phone numbers on the page. Have him identify himself, state their name, then say the code word and hang up. The less he talks, the better."

"Are the contacts awaiting his call?"

"Yes, of course, Mr. Jordan. Once Straka makes the calls, these contacts will alert key national security personnel, informing their leaders to work with the United Nations to resolve the crisis."

I thought of something again. "Wait, you and I could make these calls to the contacts on this list. Why does Nicholas have to be the one to speak with them?"

Franco Varese sighed. "Because the media, at our direction, is already placing stories about how feverishly Mr. Straka is working behind the scenes to break the stalemate," he responded. "Newspapers, television stations, blogs, cable networks, you name it. Why, he—"

"The phone lines of the contacts on this sheet of paper have voice recognition for his voice."

"How quickly you catch on," Franco Varese said, sparkling at the mastery of his scheme. "That took some doing on our part. The contacts know that his voice plus the code word activates the plan. More importantly, by actually using Straka to make the calls we add a layer of legitimacy to the entire operation."

"That is some plan."

Franco Varese clapped his approval. "It is a network extraordinaire Mr. Jordan, not my brainchild mind you, but I'm a good uncle."

"No way to prove anything," I went on, still gaming the scenario in my mind. "There is nothing incriminating whatsoever, people seemingly disconnected in hundreds of different ways from one another and in divergent continents and countries. And I imagine the phone numbers are deactivated after the plan is implemented, so there is no—"

"Trace. Exactly, Mr. Jordan, a worthless piece of paper with inoperable phone numbers. Every linkage and association with us must be hidden through layers of plausible deniability."

I said nothing and rotated my neck from side to side. To my surprise, a look of emptiness swept over his face.

"Is there something wrong?" I asked him.

Franco Varese looked past me, past the room, past the lagoon, past Miami, and finally past the world. His eyes were long into space. "We are very good at averting disaster, Mr. Jordan, this little organization of mine, the one you will soon be joining," he said, suddenly devoid of any pride. "We have painstakingly created an institute with a mandate to protect humanity from humanity, through the worst of our natures and the darkest of our motivations. We excel at that."

Once again I remained blank. I just watched him.

Franco Varese made his way to the window again. He looked deeply into the blackness. "But we still don't know *their* intentions," he said, the second time he had accentuated that thought.

"The extraterrestrials?"

I received a faraway nod. "Yes, they're a mystery," he said, peering into the nighttime sky. "So advanced and yet so simple. They intervene in only the gravest of crises. Otherwise, they leave us alone. They have their own reasons for existence, apart from ours, and to have come this far for what? I want to know those reasons, Mr. Jordan, like a lost puppy wants to find its home. We have only suppositions and theories, no real answers as to their purposes here, and very little to go on. I'm hoping you can help us learn their purposes."

"We all have our reason for existence, don't we?"

My comment brought Franco Varese back. "However do you mean?" he questioned, turning around to face me.

I inhaled deeply and took my time. "Well, we're all flowers in the field," I said, noticing his returning attention. "Different colors, different traits, all wavering in the same indifferent breeze. We're all affected the same I presume, subject to the whims of the elements, to a universe largely unfolding irrespective of our various desires and needs. I imagine every life everywhere asks the same questions, wants the same answers, ponders the same yesterdays and the many tomorrows, just like you and I."

Life is nothing if not surprises. Where I thought Franco Varese would remain glum and rather unmoved by my words, instead another blossoming unfolded across his face; what came next I never expected, but his question was a timely breath of air.

"What do you want to know here, Mr. Jordan?"

I didn't have to think very long. From somewhere deep inside of me, like a wellspring bubbling up through fractured ground, the answer came into my consciousness.

"I would like to know of love," I eventually said to him. "Everything else makes logical sense, but love is much, much different. It's bound by no physical laws. And I want to know more of it each day I live here."

Franco Varese motioned for me to come join him near the window. I did so with some curiosity. For the first time, he seemed fatherly.

"Look outside," he started persuasively, "see the sky and stars above the horizon. Before us, you see what man has built: harbors, buildings, yachts, bridges, technologies, city skyline, everything in the foreground, but beyond that is a galaxy filled with stars. Some of these stars have their own planetary systems and on some of these planets, life exists. I don't know what their worlds are like, strange to us I'm sure, but I do know on this world there is love. It defines us. It's the reason we have built all you see here. I love my wife, Mr. Jordan, and I love my children, and I love this world oftentimes more than my soul can bear. Earth is a world worth preserving, not because we humans are special in any galactic sense, but rather because our world is a world of love. Love, Mr. Jordan, love is the reason for our lives, and it must be the reason the Creator made us in the first place. Fundamentally, this little organization of ours was founded on love, to preserve our world so human love can progress to its rightful end, whatever that ending may be."

It was at that exact moment I realized this was an incredible man apart from his organization. Every lasting civilization has some denizens like him, people who transcend the best of their species and join in an elite stewardship of their planetary home. Some are driven by progress, some by mission, some by procreation, and some by service to The One. Humans, I was learning, are driven by love. With his words, I wanted to know of love all the more.

"I have felt the inklings of love," I stated, somewhat defensively. "But I do not know of its fullness. It seems as elusive to me as a butterfly. I hope someday I may hold it in my hands and finally feel its delicate wonder."

"What has stopped you?"

I shrugged my shoulders. "My directives, I suppose, well that and my duty," I said to him. "My life has been primarily about directives and duty."

"Then go do your duty, but be warned. The universe will send you the lessons of love. You can count on it. The inevitable finds us all."

We stared at each other for a time. It was the silence of appreciating another's mind. I felt his full respect and I know he felt mine.

I shook his hand and took my envelope and sheet of paper and quickly left the room. When I stepped outside I too looked deeply into the nighttime sky. Thoughts came to me like a rushing wind. I had traveled thousands of miles all over the world for what had amounted to very brief conversations with three famously brilliant minds, yet it was an unknown and diminutive Italian-born American holding the key to humankind's survival. Somehow I had found him or he had found me. He held his secret all those years and still I held mine from him. But as I walked into the moist tropical air there was one secret I had yet to discover and I prayed she was kind.

THIRTEEN

Associated Press—New York, United States
September 14, 2017

In what is being hailed as one of the great diplomatic achievements in history, United Nations Secretary General Nicholas Straka has managed to persuade the leaders of China, India, the United States, Pakistan, Australia, Japan, South Korea, Taiwan, Israel, Iran, Turkey and other countries to stand down their armies and work toward global peace. Here, and in every major city of the world, the United Nations is being described, in the words of New Zealand Prime Minister Evan Hillsborough, as an "institution of hope and action, where the dreams of humankind meet with their reality, and where our souls strive forever onward."

Separately, the militaries of China, the United States, Australia, India and Pakistan have all indicated the recent spate of UFO activity was nothing more than positioning of advanced aircraft and space based weaponry in response to changing battlefield conditions, although that explanation fails to address sightings over such diverse areas as South America, Africa, Canada and a number of other locales. The United Nations also released a statement through its Office of Public Affairs that the recent wave of UFO activity has subsided coincident with the cessation of military hostilities, apparently confirming the militaries' accounting of events.

Upon returning to my Oakland home, I rose early the following morning and walked my hills as if I had been born from this Earth. Each knoll and adjacent rise was every bit as beautiful as I remembered; I wanted to roll in the grass like a child, free and unworried and expectant for tomorrow, and it seemed like now the world would finally be different.

I might have sat on a large tree stump and contemplated the panoramic view below me for hours on end, but my cell phone rang and disturbed my blissful solitude. I glanced at the number and saw it was Nicholas.

"Well hello," I said, bantering a bit, "how good of you to call."

"Oh David, my wonderful David, I knew I could count on you," Nicholas showered on me. "What can I say? I am forever in your debt."

"Save the drama. Aristotle my ass; you must be descended from Sophocles."

He ignored me, as usual. "I can't believe you brought the world its peace," Nicholas said, nearly gasping, "as they are celebrating in the capitals of America, Europe and Asia right down to the smallest villages in Africa and Polynesia. Ghoshanad was the final piece; that madman was hours away from launching nuclear weapons when he was removed from power. I just—."

"Yes, I heard territories are being returned to their former states and all pre-war borders are being honored. Even Taiwan is free again."

"And all because of you."

"My fee for services is already in the mail."

"Anything," Nicholas brimmed, "anything you need. However did you manage to pull this off?"

"I'll never tell, so quit asking."

I knew Nicholas well enough to know he was most proud of himself. He was lavishing me, sure, but he mainly wanted to buy off my silence. He need not have worried; I couldn't tell a soul because no one would believe me and Franco Varese certainly wouldn't substantiate anything I said. Besides, I liked Nicholas, I always had, and I wasn't about to change that now. But I couldn't pass up the chance to mess with him a bit.

"There is no way to repay me and I have already contacted Newsweek for an exclusive," I said, sounding as serious as possible. "The interview is tomorrow at—"

"You bastard, don't you dare do that to me," he said, jumping from most appreciative to absolutely furious in a nanosecond. "I, I mean the United Nations, is finally at the pinnacle of its power and you want to satisfy your own selfish ego? Are you out of your mind? Listen to me, you egocentric maniac, I forbid you from taking down the United Nations for personal gain."

I doubt I have ever laughed that hard in my life. If I have, I can't remember when. I am sure Nicholas hated me then, especially when I dropped the phone and took my time climbing back onto my stump, cackling like a teenager at a sleepover.

"Don't worry, Nicholas," I finally managed, "your secret is safe with me."

The silence on the other end meant Nicholas had deduced I was conning him. His contrition was seeping through the phone like a runny faucet.

"I'm a louse, aren't I?" he asked me.

"Yes, a good louse, but you pursued every avenue to solve this crisis and for that I commend you."

Nicholas paused, a pause I remembered since our days at Williams, his mind working the silence to find a rationale for poor behavior. It was almost distinctively him.

"Well hell," he eventually said to me, "the press is eating this up. Can you blame me?"

I also knew Nicholas well enough to know he felt legitimate gratitude coupled with a heaping of emotional relief, as the crisis had been very real and his strain these past few weeks enormous. I had worried for his health. It seemed like now would be his mea culpa.

"We almost didn't make it, did we?" he asked, the gravity of the situation perhaps hitting him as we spoke further. "I want to thank you; it's just that saying such—"

"I know Nicholas and you're welcome. Now don't go getting all mushy on me."

"Well, at least let me say this," he said, a discernable gravitas in his tone. "This is hard for me, because it goes way back."

What came next was totally astounding. I had suspected this side of Nicholas, but never actually witnessed it. To this day, it still seems like a mirage.

"At Williams, I used to admire you from afar," he said, carefully choosing his words. "I wanted to act like you; I wanted to look like you; I wanted to be as popular as you; I wanted to be as smart as you. I know I am the most self-absorbed bastard on Earth and I have known that since my childhood. It's like a disease I cannot cure. But you were patient with me and overlooked my shortcomings."

"Not all of them."

The heaviness got a little lighter. "Fine, but you were there for me at Williams and you were there for me now," he said. "You are my hero, David."

I didn't know what to do. I had never related to Nicholas this way. We were being honest with each other for the first and only time and it felt very uncomfortable. There was a pit in my throat. I thought of Jenny and what she would want me to say.

"Nicholas, I have never met anyone with such a genuine concern for the downtrodden," I said to him. "You abhor injustice. You fight for human rights. You want a clean planet. I am proud to consider you my friend. I guess you could say I care for you."

I heard another pause and the shaky sound people make when their lip trembles. He was straining to find the words, any words, and after a considerable silence he spoke to me again.

"Thank you David," he said. "All I can say is thank you. You have meant the world to me."

That was the end of our conversation; I knew Nicholas must have concluded the call to keep from breaking down. That is what these humans do in such times, that much I had learned from observing people and from watching Jenny talk about her mom. I had almost felt it in myself I think, the uneasiness about your body bordering on a comfort, a feeling of peace lying just past the furthest point of your fear, and thankfully the call ended when it did. Perhaps I truly cared for Nicholas, as strange as that might seem, and perhaps if we hadn't ended the call I might have been the one who'd broken down.

Perhaps I was learning to love.

Perhaps I just was.

* * *

When I returned home, I relaxed and waited for nothing in particular. I thought Nicholas might call again or I might hear from Jenny. She would be coming home soon and would probably call me from Honolulu where she was scheduled for a brief layover. But neither phoned with any news; instead I heard a solid rap at my front door that startled me. I rose from my chair and saw through the glass it was Donald. He wore a smile as wide as the Sahara.

"Why the hell are you so happy?" I asked him.

"I'm here for my machine, so I can leave this pebble. I can't wait to get the hell out of here."

"I take it Ambassador Wren is pleased."

"You take it right, very pleased. The machine worked beyond our wildest expectations and somehow you managed to operate it without disturbing the space/time continuum."

I hated his haughtiness. "Are you kidding me?" I roared at him. "It was a couple of switches and a big blue knob. Oh, and I almost forgot, I needed an Internet connection."

Donald's face shifted to a frown. "Save the sarcasm," he told me. "All I needed was for you to leave the switches open and create a gravity field. Some wandering neighborhood kid gets sucked away to Portland and I get blamed for his disappearance."

"You are not out of the woods yet. You scratch my cabinetry and I'll have your ass."

Donald said nothing and wedged past, heading over to the machine, looking like an ugly kid miraculously kissed by a starlet. He spoke without facing me, enthralled with his device.

"Why do you value the simple woods of this tiny planet so much? A cabinet is a cabinet. The floral diversity of Earth is at the low end of the Fedlenereck Scale."

"There is as much beauty in simplicity as there is majesty in complexity. You should appreciate that; you're as simple a son of a bitch as I ever met."

"Fuck you."

I felt the urge to knock him on his ass. Another cross word and I would. "Your machine, your drinking, and your subservience to Ambassador Wren are about as complicated as an amoeba living in some backwater pond," I said, baiting him. "Quite frankly, I would rather have the amoeba's life."

Donald turned and faced me. I was hoping he'd find the courage to take a swing at me, but he didn't. He did what he always did when I was mad at him; he made nice.

"Look, I apologize if I insulted you regarding your operation of the machine," he said, in a much softer tone. "I promise not to scratch your cabinetry. I actually came to thank you for a job well done. I can now escape the dead eyes."

I eased down, feeling sorry for him. He really didn't have much in life other than his drinking. "They're not dead eyes," I finally said to him. "Humans don't have our golden sparkles, our own distinctive evolutionary trait, but their emotional states run much deeper than our own."

Donald went suddenly aghast. "You felt what these simpletons feel?" he asked.

I straightened and looked at him without blinking. "I have, but only peripherally," I answered, judging Donald's reaction. "I made a judgment call and felt it was worth the risk. Actually, I couldn't help myself."

"But Ambassador Wren warned against dabbling in human emotion. Remember the Abstron Code."

The Abstron Code is a principle of respect for other cultures, signed by most interstellar travelers. The Abstron Machile is the most spiritually advanced race in the galaxy, and their code, while relatively brief, is sheer brilliance. The primary tenet advises against incorporating the ways of other cultures as it is a disservice to both.

"We take enough risk here," Donald added firmly. "Aging pills, digestive enhancement, gravity equalizer phasing, all so we can function at a high level. But to experiment in human emotion is way past cause. I think you may be crazy. Why the hell would you risk it?"

My next comments would be chancy, but I made them anyway. "Because maybe we're missing something. Love may be the grandest prize in the universe."

"But it is forbidden."

"I know."

"But it is forbidden."

"You already said that."

Donald stared hard at me. He seemed to weigh the consequences. "Fine, but we never had this conversation," he said, scanning me for agreement. "I don't need to be an accomplice to human emotion. Ambassador Wren will have me exiled to Quadrant 8. I'll just get my equipment and go."

I watched as Donald carried his prized machine out to his car. He actually waved goodbye and I waved back at him. My cabinetry was unscathed, but I gave it a good polishing anyway. When Donald drove away, I figured it was the last I would see of him. He would probably be summoned. We had a strange relationship, one clearly strained and often adversarial, but we had worked together for a long time here on Earth and I had to admit a part of me felt guilty for not being kinder to him. Unexpectedly, I wished him well.

*   *   *

As I gazed out onto the hillside the grasses swayed golden in the breezes, so I opened up the windows and welcomed the airy freshness into my home. I made toast and honey for my breakfast and checked my email. Nothing. No correspondence at all. Indian summer was in the day, the Bay Area weather warming to its usual short sleeve weather of early fall. Things should have been fine. Instead, I felt a strange uneasiness about the morning. I stepped outside. The neighbor's dog chased a cat up a fencepost, barking his usual salvo at me, before sauntering back into his yard and panting. I never liked that dog much. And although his antics were familiar, they did little to calm my apprehension. I wondered again if my long exposure on Earth was causing brain degeneration because something was clearly wrong.

Still, I couldn't quite place it. I piddled in the yard, accomplishing nothing, finally pacing and then pacing some more before returning inside.

After awhile, I showered and clicked on the headline news.

It was then I saw the cause of my distress.

A dour newswoman reported a plane crash in the Pacific from some kind of terrorist attack; one hundred and thirty nine people killed when the jet exploded mid-flight somewhere near the Hawaiian Islands. The satellite relay showed bodies and baggage bobbing in the swells. I thought *no, it can't be, there is simply no way.* I tried Jenny's number, but it went directly into voicemail.

I watched the names of the victims appear on the television. There were none that I recognized. The reporter noted the list was incomplete waiting notification of relatives, but names were trickling in and when more names came through she would report them. I sat glued to the television. A big truck rumbled outside and then went further down the road.

The reporter was about halfway through the names of the victims when I saw something flash on the bottom of the screen. It was like someone took a wooden log and swung it into my body. It was there in bold white letters, the newswoman quickly confirming the name: *Jenny Scott Wright.* Jenny was dead.

I staggered outside and crumbled into a ball, losing sense of my surroundings. I couldn't hear a thing. I rolled onto my lawn and cried big, dripping tears from someplace deep inside of me that had previously never existed. I still don't know where the tears came from. I shook hard once and finally what was left of me faced the emptiness of the sky.

"Jenny," I screamed into the void.

My tears grew bigger with each passing moment. *Please pain, please go away. I can't take you anymore.* I vomited my breakfast onto the ground and gagged until I thought my throat would crack. The neighbor's dog was at my fence, jumping and barking fiercely, but he made no sound. Somehow, I wobbled my way up and tottered into the woods and fell into some thickly brush. Blood ran down my arms and face, but I walked until I stumbled again.

I don't know what happened next or how I came into the circle of cottonwoods, but when I found myself I was on the ground and crying her name. I clawed at the dirt and soon all the sounds of nature returned. I felt Jenny all around me. The sun poured in through seams of the forest, flooding the loam in a soft and delicate light.

"So this is love?" I cried to the wind.

I must have passed out for a time, but when I regained consciousness my arms stung and I felt moistened dust all over my face. I ached everywhere. Where I am from it is said The One can send a message from the departed if you listen to a world at its quietest. So I cleared my mind and waited for nature to speak.

It didn't take long. I smelled the coconut and berry scents of Jenny's hair and her words to me were unmistakable.

"Love again," she said softly.

Something passed through the cottonwoods and I knew Jenny's soul had gone on. A world gone mad and a crisis just past mattered little to me anymore, nor did my duty or what to do with my life. I felt the emptiness of an abyss. The last I remembered I rolled back over onto the ground and thought of Jenny and all we had known. To this day, I do not know how I made it back to my home in the woods but when I did the darkness filled my home and I was alone.

FOURTEEN

San Francisco Chronicle—San Francisco, California
March 8, 2018
*It has been nearly six months since the easing of world tensions and it is fair
to say the Earth has entered into a Pax Globalis, a golden era of peace and
cooperation unprecedented in all of human history. United Nations Secretary
General Nicholas Straka, whose leadership is credited with finally achieving
the mission of this often criticized and ridiculed body of world government,
is revered in every corner of the Earth and this man of Everyman has entered
the pantheon of the great statesmen of history.*

I never knew six months could last so long. My memories of Jenny
were with me every day of my pain. Gradually, as time ensures, a healing
process began and I eventually tasted my food again and enjoyed the sweet
sounds of music and my walks alone in the woods. Fog became a cooling
friend instead of a suffocating blanket and I often smiled at the deer. Still,
when the hills were at their quietest I thought of Jenny and cried until my
eyes burned. One morning I missed her so much I had to walk faster to
keep from falling over. I know I still love her. I always will. I hope Jenny will
forgive me, but I never want to love again.

Donald had been reassigned soon after Jenny died. I never met with
Ambassador Wren; well, not until this morning anyway when I looked out
past my front porch and saw him standing straightway in the sun. His presence caught me by surprise.

"Please come in," I said to him, pulling open the door.

"Thank you," he said in return. "I hope you don't mind seeing me."

"No, of course not. It's been a long time."

Ambassador Wren looked me over. "Yes, much too long," he said, seconding my comment. "Unfortunately, that is the nature of my position."

I hadn't seen Ambassador Wren since I was a young man, when I first came to the Earth. His demeanor, always courteous and forthright, hadn't changed and his posture, rigid and professional, quickly came back to me; I remembered thinking of him as a kind of statue being in my youth, almost intimidating in his stance, offset only by his civility and periodic smile.

I motioned for him to sit on my couch, but instead he wandered into the library and took a seat at the head chair. I joined him in the room and sat on the couch and faced him. Terseness filled the air.

"You have performed magnificently here," Ambassador Wren stated. "You are deeply situated and not a single human suspects you of a thing. Finding Franco Varese and his organization was an especially fortuitous discovery. The Council is very proud of you."

"Thank you."

"These humans have ceased hostilities and are beginning to see themselves as one people," he said, studying me. "We are all pleasantly surprised."

"And justice?"

Ambassador Wren reached for a mint and put one into his mouth. "Their next stage will be to extend rights to everyone," he said, offering me a mint. I smiled to myself remembering that he had loved mints all those years before. He obviously still did. "This will accelerate their path toward harmony with themselves and should limit wars and thus our involvement," he noted.

I relaxed and leaned back. "Then I will enjoy staying here," I said.

Ambassador Wren swallowed hard. "I could send you back, you know. The Council advised it. But perhaps you still have some services to perform."

I blinked at him curiously. "What services?" I asked.

"Well for one, this Straka character may self-destruct at any time. We need you to cultivate a replacement and form him to our wishes, as you did with Straka in his academic years."

"They still choose, you know. His own life choices could have led him toward another path."

"Of course they choose. It is forbidden by The One to interfere with free will. Molding, however, is quite appropriate and you molded Straka into highly predictable paths. He never knew of the night sessions, did he?"

"No, he never suspected nor had any recollections."

"That is excellent," Ambassador Wren said, nodding. "How many did you perform?"

"Nine. The last session was the most effective."

"Then we will continue to select humans of stature and influence and presumed influence. We are pretty adroit at that task and have been quite successful in the last twenty years or so."

"As you wish."

Ambassador Wren suddenly stiffened. "Donald Niebauer told us of your experiment with human emotion, once he was safely reassigned," he said. "That was imprudent of you and careless."

"Donald a rat? What a shock."

Ambassador Wren cleared his throat. "Don't hold that against him; he's loyal to me," he said. "Since you survived this journalist woman's death, The Council is interested in having you delve further into the phenomenon of love. Because of you, we have changed our rules. You should feel honored."

"Honored?" I shouted sarcastically, nearly coming off the couch. "Because of our wars with the Illick, Jenny is dead. I had visions of my suffering long before she died because love is that powerful. I have learned all my presentiments resulted from love. Human authorities never found a terrorist link to her plane crash, nor any mechanical failure. It was Eric Waller, I know it."

Ambassador Wren didn't have to say anything; his look concurred with my assessment. But as was his way, he spoke nevertheless. "It was Waller's way of evening the score," he said to me. "We at The Council surmised that as well. But you evened the score again. We placed another implant into Waller's brain at Aueretern. Your hunch was right. My sympathies regarding the woman, but we need you to explore love for us."

I glanced past my superior. "No, I won't go through that again," I said to him. "And you can't make me."

Ambassador Wren paused to gather his thoughts. He relaxed his posture. "It might be important to our relations here," he said amiably, trying to placate me. "Soon, humans will become aware of our existence; some of their leadership is already apprised."

"There are countless books written about love and—"

"None by us. We want a direct appraisal. You're in the best position to provide such an assessment."

I shook my head. For some reason speaking of Jenny made me angry with him. "Spoken like a true clinician," I said condescendingly, "only you don't understand love or how it functions. You can't make love happen. It finds you and graces you with its presence. It's a gift these people welcome and one we reject in the name of progress. And it is we who have suffered because of it."

"That is blasphemy," Ambassador Wren said, his voice rising. "The Council made a decision to eliminate primary feelings because they cause war and suffering. Our struggles with the Illick result from their failure to make the same choice. Look at how far we've come as a people."

I had to laugh. Living among humans had taught me of their virtues, love being their greatest. I had learned that much about the peculiar race that abides here, albeit the hard way.

"Have you wondered why our eyes sparkle?" I eventually asked him.

"No, our sparkles result from centuries of DNA manipulation to eliminate primary feelings."

"How about the hollowness we feel during sexual relations even though we experience physical pleasure?"

"Yes, we know that as well. What is your point?"

I delivered the coup de grace with a satisfaction I never suspected. My years on Earth had taught me the lesson I sought since my childhood.

"Our sparkles are the residue of our former selves," I said. "The love we once felt had to go somewhere and it went into our eyes. We are hollow in sex because our soul is no longer full."

"That again is blasphemy! I could have you banished to the furthest reaches. You are special among us, gifted like few others, so think before you speak to me this way again."

"I have thought," I said without hesitation, surprising myself with my calm, "and I will cultivate a replacement for Nicholas Straka and that is all I will do for you. Love I keep to myself and you will have no say in my feelings or what I do with them."

There was a long pause as Ambassador Wren sought to defuse the situation. I saw he didn't want to face The Council for my insurrection. "You work for us, never forget that about yourself," he said, his face slackening.

"I am forever changed, so never forget that about me. I am no longer the boy you sent here so many years ago."

Ambassador Wren clasped his hands together. Frustration filled his eyes. "Be reasonable, you're a hero to most of the galaxy," he pleaded with me. "Never throw that away."

I came and stood directly in his face. I felt the apprehension surging through his body. I watched his eyes as he watched me.

"I will not love again but I will tell you what I know of love. Never ask me this request again. Are we clear on that?"

Ambassador Wren gulped hard once more. I was insubordinate, but he overlooked it. His eyes danced away from mine, but they caught me again when he spoke.

"I will inform The Council it's not possible for you to grant our request but that you'll debrief us on your experience with love and cultivate a replacement for Nicholas Straka," he said, his eyes seeking confirmation. "It already tells me much of this love, you choosing never to love again. And because of love you are willing to disobey me."

I put my hand on his shoulder in a disarming manner. It was the right time for such a gesture.

"Remember as children when we each beheld the sky of the Simeol?" I asked him. The Simeol is an equator location on our planet where a confluence of atmospheric conditions causes light to be fractionalized revealing the full spectrum as one panoramic experience filling the entire sky. It is unique in the galaxy.

Ambassador Wren nodded. He seemed suddenly tranquil. "Yes I do," he said in reminiscence. "For the first moment of discovery we have taken each child to that view in our world. It is the greatest enjoyment we know."

"Well not quite, for it's nothing compared to love. Love is beyond the beyond and far beyond that. It is everything worth living for and then as much beyond everything as the mind can imagine."

Ambassador Wren bowed his head and then looked up at me quizzically. "But how can this be?" he asked me. "These humans are so primitive compared to our people, so warring and so far behind us."

"Their love is connected with their progress, so they experience totality. We need that as well."

A light went on in Ambassador Wren's head. I saw it in his eyes. "Do you mean we might feel our advancement?" he asked me.

"Yes, that's it exactly, it's called appreciation and it's wonderful. You must try it sometime."

"Did you appreciate her?"

The suddenness of his question stopped me cold. My eyes filled with tears.

"Yes, more than anyone could possibly know," I said. "Her love for me caused appreciation."

Ambassador Wren gazed at me quizzically. He wanted to understand, I felt that in him, but he hadn't lived among these humans and didn't know the qualities of love. It must have scared him to see me cry.

Ambassador Wren took a deep breath and held me in his sight. He spoke very softly. "I wish I had experienced such a thing," he said, before turning and making his way to a clearing in the woods. He looked back at me before the light beam came and nodded a goodbye. I watched him disappear in peace.

I never saw him again. He was replaced by a much younger ambassador who largely gave me free reign. I heard Ambassador Wren finally went home to our planet after years of dutiful service and I also heard he spent much of his time reading the history of Earth and its paradoxical people. Strangely, I think of him now and again.

These days I walk my hills and go about my duties, but I think of Jenny often and at times she is still with me. I love her as much as before. I know I always will. I never want to leave this tiny blue planet encircling its smallish pale star because it's where Jenny lived and as long as I am here she is not far from me. When I am low and question the reasons for living I think of her and remember love and her laughing along with me. Jenny always made me smile. I have learned that is the best of love, smiling and laughing together, counting on one another. In what is left of my life now, remembering her and her smiling along with me passes for happiness, and when I walk my hills I am grateful for her and for the truth of these people as I have learned it.